THE BILLIONAIRE'S GIFT

A SPIRITUAL BUSINESS PARABLE

Edward Iwata

Jared + Z

Thanks for the friendliest
+ best coffe bar in Silicon
Valley!

Ed Iwata
8/10/13

1

Book Cover Art and Design: KitFosterDesign.com.
Book Layout ©2013 BookDesignTemplates.com.

The Billionaire's Gift/ Edward Iwata – 1st ed.
ISBN-13: 978-1490916545
ISBN-10: 1490916547
ASIN: B00CYR 4AMQ

Please contact the author at info@EdwardIwata.com

To all who give and serve others, often at great cost. Your good works inspire us.

Thank you.

"We know that every moment is a moment of grace, every hour an offering . . . ."

—ELIE WIESEL, AUTHOR.[1]

"I've always been told that you are given a blessing to be a blessing."

—NE-YO, SINGER.[2]

"I believe we have more caring than we know what to do with."

—BILL GATES, TECHNOLOGIST[3]

"Lord, make me an instrument of Thy peace . . . For it is in giving that we receive . . . And it is in dying that we are born to eternal life. Amen."

—"PEACE PRAYER,"
SAINT FRANCIS OF ASSISI.[4]

Contents

Prologue

DAMN THE BILLIONAIRE, he swears. F-ck his greedy punk ass.

The maintenance man is parked in the cavernous garage of a downtown high-rise. Since hearing the news from the billionaire's hatchet men that he and five thousand coworkers will lose their jobs, he has sat in his truck for nearly twenty-four hours.

Not moving. Not sleeping. Not eating or drinking.

He cannot tell whether the sun is rising or setting. Whether the foul taste in his dry mouth is blood or cheap wine. Whether the pounding in his head is his heartbeat, or a laborer's jackhammer down the street.

His breath reeks. His cracked lips sting and bleed, and he cannot swallow. Sweat sticks to his skin like stale beer. Urine soaks his dank pants. He smells of that old man's odor, the stench of fetid, fleshy decay.

As the parking garage empties at night, a bored security guard drives by, ignoring the maintenance man's familiar white truck.

Age spots blot the bald spot on the maintenance man's head. Deep wrinkles erode his face, and the sun and cleaning chemicals have corroded his skin. When he stretches, his knees lock, as if welded at the joints. He howls in pain, like a dog struck by a car.

Despite his dried bones, the maintenance man still can conjure vivid memories from his youth. Flirty waitresses at his favorite diner called him a Robert Redford with muscles, long before he lost his lush hair and grew large, saggy breasts. After the military and trade school, the maintenance man found plenty of girls. But he couldn't find work, so he lived for months on the streets.

In the steel-and-concrete valleys of the financial district, the maintenance man felt like an explorer, a *conquistador,* for a week or two. Then it got worse. Scuttling like a rat down deserted alleys. Eating rotten food from dumpsters. Crapping in bushes and vacant lots. Begging for coins to buy smokes and T-Bird wine. On cold nights, the maintenance man slept near steam vents. Or he sat through church sermons in exchange for a hot meal and shelter. At the soup kitchen with the tastiest spaghetti and the firmest Army cots, a fire-and-brimstone pastor with rheumy eyes waved his Bible in search of stray souls. *Remember,* he preached, *the Lord loves each and every one of you!*

Luckily for the maintenance man, another military vet at the billionaire's company took a chance and hired him off the streets. The summer gig turned into a lifelong job.

Each day, the maintenance man shuffles from floor to floor, fixing lights and scrubbing toilets for the smug suits that skirt past him. Some flash fake smiles or pretend not to see him, while others act as if he has leprosy or some Asian bird virus. One guy shoots the breeze as he pisses.

"You catch the game last night, bro'?" he says, zipping up his pants and taking a mobile call before the maintenance man even replies.

Arrogant, ungrateful pricks. The maintenance man fought in Vietnam for their free-market right to make heaps of money. More power to the money men if they make a good, honest living. But blue-collar folks and military vets built this country. The rich dickheads aren't entitled to frag his ass when he hits his sixties. They can't piss away his retirement money in foreign countries, and then dump him in the streets without even a handshake.

That wasn't the deal.

The labor union protests the mass cuts, but can do nothing to stop companies from shipping jobs and assets abroad. Even a strike vote and walkout threat accomplished nothing last year, when the suits chopped benefits and pay hikes anyway.

That killed the workers' spirits.

Every day the rich men come and go, talking of cash and capital flow. The maintenance man has worked for them for forty freaking years. Measuring his life in coffee breaks, spitting out butt-ends of wasted days and unseen ways.[5] And then it's screw you buddy, enjoy your sunset years. One less old guy to accommodate in the workforce.

Well, the party isn't over, he thinks.

When his graveyard shift starts at midnight, the maintenance man winces and steps from his truck.

He hauls a heavy tool cart from his truck bed and rolls it into the service elevator, getting off at the lobby. Still wearing his dark gray uniform and employee's badge from yesterday, he nods to the security guards.

"What's up?" says one guard.

"Same old, same old," says the maintenance man. "Work, eat, sleep. Work, eat, sleep."

"I hear you, brother. Life's like that, but we gotta deal. Hope you didn't get a pink slip."

Grunting, the maintenance man pushes his tool cart into the elevator. The elevator rises rapidly, and he exits on the thirtieth floor. The entire floor is used by the billionaire, the fabled CEO of a well-known global company.

No one is working late. The maintenance man has to hurry, though.

He trudges down a long, marbled hallway that echoes with each step. Sphinx-like busts of former chairmen flank the hall.[6] They rule with stares of smug command, like royalty in a godless land. The hallway stretches far to the billionaire's office suite, cut off from all but his top executives and his secretary.

Inside the billionaire's office, the maintenance man eyeballs the tycoon's lustrous, custom-made desk. Handcrafted from fine Brazilian and African woods, the desk was shipped to America as carefully as a concert grand piano

Cursing the billionaire, the maintenance man gives a big shove to the tool cart, smashing it into the desk. The heavy desk cracks, but doesn't shatter.

The maintenance man grabs a rusty towing chain that has sat in his truck and tool cart for years, piled with other grimy gear that he bought with his own wages.

Lugging the chain, he swings it repeatedly at the desk, gouging and gashing the fine wood. Then he gift-wraps the billionaire's desk in a heavy steel bow. A present for the man who has everything.

Before security can respond, the maintenance man grabs a blowtorch and fires it up, then aims at the desk. Sparks singe his unprotected face and arms. Within seconds, the blowtorch's three-thousand-degree flame scorches the desk into a smoky, blackened mass.

Known as a thorough worker, the maintenance man also roasts a leather sofa and armchair. Then he charbroils an oak conference table, a coffee table, an antique secretary desk.

He stares at the billionaire's custom glass-door bookcase, filled with fine editions of twentieth century literature, from Hemingway novels to Dante translations. The billionaire's books are as precious to him as his money. Barbecuing the brittle tomes will be the best revenge.

As the maintenance man lifts the blowtorch, the fire alarm and emergency sprinklers suddenly go off. The force of the spray surprises him. The water quickly douses the smoldering furniture and soaks the maintenance man.

Choking on smoke and embers, he curses and dumps the blowtorch on the waterlogged carpet.

Down the hall, elevator lights blink. Security guards will be there soon.

For his finishing touch, the maintenance man quickly hammers a large wooden sign on the billionaire's door. Painted in crimson flames and Gothic black lettering, the sign reads:

Go to Hell, You Bastard.
May You Die In More Pain
Than The Pain You Inflict On Others.
No Forgiveness, No Repentance.

The maintenance man steps back to admire his work.

"It ain't Rembrandt, but I'll take it," he says. "I should have listened to you, Mom, and gone to art school."

The maintenance man plops on the billionaire's chair, and stretches his legs on the desk. Closest he'll ever get to this ass-wipe, he thinks, spitting on the carpet.

He cleans the billionaire's private bathroom every night, even dumping a load there now and then, and the man doesn't even know he exists.

Striking a match, the maintenance man lights up a pricy cigar that he had been saving for early retirement next year. No gold watches and golden parachutes for janitors and secretaries, so a nice smoke will have to do.

The security guards rush into the office suite.

"What are you doin'?" one says. "You crazy?"

"Just a little gift for Mr. Billionaire," the maintenance man says. "The shithead deserves it. All union brothers and

11

sisters in agreement, raise your hands. All who disagree can kiss my fired ass, and five thousand others."

CHAPTER ONE

The Billionaire

"Then I looked on all the works that my hands had wrought . . . and, behold, all was vanity and vexation of spirit, and there was no profit under the sun."

—ECCLESIASTES 2:11, *THE BIBLE.*[7]

THAT'S THE SPIRIT, the billionaire thinks, when he sees the hand-painted sign. An artistic, literate janitor. That's why he's so mad. He's under-employed. He should be writing speeches for executives.

The billionaire wants to keep the sign as a memento, but the police need it as evidence. He also wants to finish grilling the conference table, but the cops tell him not to risk a fire. A law-and-order kind of guy, the billionaire lets the cops take a photo of him wielding the blowtorch, snarling at the camera.

"Thank you, sir," says a young officer. "This goes next to my baseball trophies and my Dad's Bronze Star."

"Vietnam?" the billionaire says.

"Yes sir."

"I missed Vietnam for medical reasons, but my father fought in Europe in World War II. Make sure you thank your Dad for his service."

"Will do."

To the cops' surprise, the billionaire does not press criminal charges against the maintenance man, even though the destruction of property could have led to a disastrous blaze.

His secretary, the first startled employee to walk into the office early that morning, urges him to file charges. The police say that the secretary would make an excellent witness – calm, reliable, trustworthy.

But the billionaire does not want to waste his time, or risk getting dragged into court. He has a company to run. To cover part of the damages to his office, he uses money that would have gone to the maintenance man's severance pay. If his union wants to file a complaint, so be it.

The media slap a nickname on the billionaire: the Blowtorch.

The nickname fits. The billionaire's slash-and-burn style angers many. Sacrificing the workforce is the easiest way to boost his company's financials during downturns.

The downside for the billionaire: after each round of layoffs, he fields a round of anonymous death threats. The threats at first alarmed him. But four decades of deal-making and risk-taking have toughened his rhino-like hide.

"Comes with the job description," he tells the cops.

His secretary never gets used to it, though. Each time she screens a threatening phone call or e-mail, she warns her boss to be careful. Most are empty threats, but all it takes is one mad gunman.

"Don't worry about it," he tells her. "Security does a good job."

Besides, the billionaire has his handgun, legally hidden under his coat. He uses his favorite hunting rifle to take bears, wild hogs, and other dangerous game. Aiming a small handgun indoors is a bit tougher for him. He is a decent shot, though. Good enough to defend himself against rabid workers and other nut jobs.

"You know how to use that firearm, sir?" says a young, tattooed guard.

"You know how to run a company?" the billionaire says. "I was shooting before your cousin gave birth to you."

The local police and corporate security, teeming with former FBI and Secret Service agents, take the threats seriously. Armed guards cover all entrances. Police detectives question bitter rivals and workers. Corporate security clears each visitor, checks each phone call and e-mail. Security makes the billionaire change his daily driving routine, and they escort him nearly everywhere. One

15

morning, employees see a police dog hunting for explosives in the company's parking garage.

At night, a security guard parks outside the billionaire's coastal home, a short hike from the ocean and a large bridge that spans the harbor strait.

"We'd hate to see anything happen to you," his security chief says.

"Don't mind my grousing," the billionaire says. "You gents are well worth your salaries."

Even with the precautions, corporate security advises the billionaire to play it safe by hiring a personal bodyguard.

"A private bodyguard?" he says. "Think I'm rich?"

Business magazines and Wall Street analysts peg the billionaire's wealth at $2 billion to $2.5 billion. Close enough, the billionaire thinks.

Small change by New World standards. The moneyed stratosphere is getting crowded. *Forbes* counts more than one thousand global billionaires, with many in China and India passing slack-jawed Westerners.

The billionaire snorts. It used to be a badge of prestige to be a millionaire with an "m." But now, given hyper-globalization and the monetization of the planet, a million bucks wouldn't last a day.

As a college student during the post-World War II boom, the billionaire scoffed at a popular TV show in which a millionaire handed $1 million to shocked strangers on the streets. He didn't know who was sadder: the bleeding-heart millionaire who doled out money to ease his guilt, or the TV viewers praying to win the lottery.

The billionaire cannot imagine giving handouts in the world's mega-slums, ruled by armies of rats and roaches. Without security, he wouldn't last longer than a few heartbeats. The locals would beat him and strip him of his clothes, fight for his gold watch and dress shoes, then sell the assets on the black market. The nuns and tree-huggers who buy stock in his company to attend shareholders' meetings would call this racist, but he calls it brutal, Malthusian reality. A model of emerging market-efficiency amid sparse resources and too many Hottentots to feed, he thinks. Shipments of condoms would do more humanitarian good than food and medicine, which get hijacked anyway.

Once, the billionaire witnessed a fatal beating in an overseas slum. Heading to back to his hotel, he and his driver heard shouting a block away. Passing an intersection, they saw it. The beating started slowly, then grew more frenzied as the crowd got larger. The victim tried to run, but fell and curled into a ball on the ground, before lying still. As the billionaire's car sped off, the horde stuffed an old tire over the victim's head, then set the tire on fire in a necklace of flames. Fortunately, the victim already was dead. The billionaire and his driver had a clear view of the killers. The driver recognized one of the attackers – a street thug seen often in the area.

"Sir," the driver said, "we need to report this."

"No, keep going," the billionaire said. "There's nothing we can do. The police here won't investigate anything."

In the cruel calculus of business and politics, life is cheaper in much of the world. Poor folks are valued less from cradle to grave, in modern and developing nations alike. Doctors and insurers, generals and soldiers, presidents and prime ministers – all play God, all weigh the value of lives in their work. Why shouldn't the billionaire?

Even if he wanted to, he couldn't save the world anyway. His assets for altruism are puny, compared to others. He'll leave the health of nations to do-gooders like Bill Gates, Warren Buffett, and their Billionaire Boy Scouts.

God bless 'em, the billionaire thinks, but he'll stick to what he does best: building his business.

From day one, the billionaire's century-old company has been blessed by the profit gods.

It has survived economic catastrophes and market crashes that doomed other corporations, and its sure and steady growth has intrigued long-run investors from New York to New Delhi.

The business was founded by the billionaire's grandparents, European immigrants who sweated for years on farms, mills, and meat-packing plants in the Midwestern region of America. Seeking an easier livelihood, the grandparents prayed for their family's safety and moved to a major port city and bay, and they bought a small general-goods store in the downtown's financial district.

Their timing was auspicious. The city was rebuilding in the early twentieth century after a once-in-a-lifetime storm and flooding destroyed much of the town. The store thrived, drawing everyone from laborers to socialites.

When the billionaire's grandparents retired, his parents ran the business during the pre-World War II era. They did not know that the war and the ensuing decades would lead to the greatest economic growth in the history of mankind. They stayed near the financial district, a kind of mini-Wall Street. The region's bankers and their financial firepower lit up the state's multibillion-dollar economy.

Like prophets, the billionaire's parents foresaw that more money would surge across global borders in the coming years. So they sold their retail company and took a wise leap of faith into international trade, rapidly building a small business empire. Their specialty was shipping agricultural products to starving countries. Today, emerging nations and multinationals use the company's global model for goods of all kinds, from medicine to television sets.

After his parents retired and died, the billionaire took over the company. He envisaged that another vast wave of globalization – ignited by finance, technology, and the spread of Western business practices – would shake the world, as China, India, Russia, and Latin America unleashed their economies.

Poorer socialist countries fall in love with the capitalist revolution as soon as they see that money isn't evil, the billionaire tells potential investors.

"You know what's evil?" he says. "Poverty and starvation are evil. Squatting to shit in holes in the ground is evil. Hell, in some of those slums, when the street kids aren't begging for money, they're crapping like animals on the road."

The billionaire shakes his head. The new global elites better get the running water and sewage going before they build those economic kingdoms that are supposed to kick America's ass. Christ, haven't they heard of cholera and malaria, epidemics and pandemics? They need to buy more mosquito nets from Gates and Buffett.

"That's so condescending," says a woman from a socially-responsible investment fund, over her fixed-price dinner and a bottle of fine wine.

"Condescending?" the billionaire says. "Have you ever gone window-shopping in a *favela* in Rio? Makes our slums look like Fifth Avenue. They need more capitalist running dogs like me in there. We'll give them more opportunities than a million social justice programs. Amen to rich men."

Of course, the billionaire's wealth came without the Third World hardships. After inheriting a huge chunk of change from his father, the rest, to his credit, came from his own business and investment daring and resolve.

For sure, the billionaire's parents raised an honest boy. He doesn't deal on the side, doling out business favors to family and friends. He doesn't hide corporate money in fishy investment vehicles. He doesn't borrow the corporate jet for long weekends in Europe and the tropics.

But he still is as cold and as cunning as they come.

There are the big bets against firms that look ripe and healthy to others, but that the billionaire suspects are rotting at the core.

There are insider shares in tech startups that he sells at the market's peak – just before the stock price falls like geese hit by buckshot. His venture investments, from Nasdaq in New York to the *Novo Mercado* in Brazil, swept the billionaire into the global elite of wealth holders.

There is his high CEO pay, pegged to his company's growth in sales, stock price, market share, investment returns. His pay is well-deserved in good years. But even when the company trails competitors, the billionaire still earns many millions of undeserved dollars.

The mergers also are a godsend. Not the megamergers that rock the stock market and always fail, enriching only bankers and attorneys. Rather, the billionaire prowls for smaller $100 million to $400 million deals that fly under the media radar.

"Like catching fish in a pond," he says.

Then there is the gold and silver. The billionaire is a precious-metals fanatic. And gold has been the most universal medium of exchange in ancient and modern times alike. It doesn't burn or decay. Large-scale gold heists are rare. And everyone wants some.

"Take your pick, boys," the billionaire says. "A mountain of bullion, or another hyped-up Internet stock?"

Only his longtime secretary, his legal and financial advisors, and a few others know about the gold bars and coins. The king-making capitalists of the world won't base the global money supply on gold. So the billionaire and a handful of partners have hoarded their personal reserves. Some show off their affluence in mansions, museums, and other temples of wealth. The billionaire prefers to hide his fortune.

To spread the risk, the gold is stashed from Switzerland to Saudi Arabia. In America, the billionaire and his partners use three small underground vaults to store their treasures. One vault is buried deep in the Nevada desert, next to an old missile silo sold to a commercial property firm owned by the billionaire's people. Another vault is under the pine forests of California, near an old Gold Rush ghost town bought by a land preservation foundation run by proxies for the billionaire. The last vault is hidden on a mountainside in Colorado, near a firebreak on the billionaire's ranch.

Getting the gold trucked quietly to the vaults was harder than breaking into foreign markets. The billionaire used three different gold-hauling crews, so each team only knew their cargo's destination. They earned a pile of cash, paid to them in smaller yearly chunks, like a lottery jackpot. The payments will continue as long as the vaults stay secret.

"If you talk, the money walks," the billionaire's people told the crews.

So far, no one has talked.

The vaults do not seem extreme to the billionaire, who is old enough to remember the Cold War and the Cuban Missile Crisis. As a teenager, he helped his father turn their basement into an A-bomb shelter, stocking it with food, water, medical supplies, firearms, and ammunition.

That was another world, another epoch. The dinosaur age in Internet time. Now, everything has flipped inside-out. The global economy reigns. And anyone who doesn't leap aboard will end up like cockroach fossils in rock and resin.

"Atlas isn't shrugging," the billionaire says. "He's tilting the whole damn planet."

Surprisingly, some still don't believe in the shifting economic tides. So each spring, the billionaire has to sell globalization to reluctant shareholders over drinks and dinner.

He entertains them in the presidential suite of a ritzy downtown hotel. The high-rise view of his fairy-tale city and harbor always helps his marketing pitch. More than one investor has been seduced by the sparkling night scenery.

The billionaire's home state long has been a pillar of the world's economy. Many of his shareholders – pension funds, mutual funds, wealthy individuals – started investing abroad decades ago, when finance and technology began smashing borders faster than any armies.

But gun-shy investors need more persuading before they pour billions of dollars into foreign nations that may or may not be America's allies, depending on the latest trade deals and White House occupants.

The billionaire's secretary, who is better with people than her crusty boss, suggests that he win over investors by appealing to their common human values. He takes her advice, but also appeals to their common love of money.

"Listen, I'm as patriotic as the next guy," the billionaire says in a welcoming talk before dinner. "So trust me when I say that many foreign investors speak our *lingua franca*.

"Just like us, they have families to feed. Just like us, they enjoy the fruits of their labors. Just like us, they want value and growth in their investments.

"Demographics are destiny, and all of the flag-waving in the world won't slow global trade. A buck and a pound no longer make the world go 'round. The new coins of the realm? *Yuan* and *rubles*. Everyone loves the colors of currency and the sound of money, *ka-ching, ka-ching*.

"It is what it is, is it not? At the end of the day, wealth always has been the great equalizer."

Given his passion for corporate conquests, the billionaire is an avid reader of military history and a collector of battlefield relics, from the U.S. Army steel pot helmet on his office desk, to the glinting nineteenth century *katana,* or *samurai* sword, displayed on his wall.

The scarred helmet came from a late board director, a general who had fought in Europe as a young soldier during

World War II. His helmet, the general had said, carries the souls and prayers of his buddies who had died in battle.

The sword came from a British art collector, who had bought it from a Japanese auto executive, who had bought it from a master metal-smith and *katana* maker. The *katana* maker had said that his great-grandfather had carved ocean waves on the scabbard because the sword's spirit always looked to the sea.

Like many hard-driving executives, the billionaire fancies himself a corporate warrior. It's a cheap metaphor. But big business truly is akin to war. There is epic bloodshed. There are victors and the vanquished. And the prizes are wealth, power, and buildings named after the triumphant.

The billionaire's mergers and takeovers resemble military campaigns. Onward, corporate soldiers. In his domain, there are no just and moral crusades on behalf of the righteous. It is combat, pure and simple.

"There's blood in the trenches," he tells an investor, "and it sure ain't mine."

His tactics are cutthroat.

He buys rival firms by attacking their weakest point, the chinks in their business armor, whether poor products, small markets, clueless executives, unhappy investors – often all of the above.

Or he joins forces with another strong rival or investor, forming a powerful pincer that crushes the target if it does not succumb.

More stealthily, his corporate spies plant harmful market rumors, steal business and research secrets, recruit key executives and other talent. Eventually, the rival business rots and collapses from the inside.

If all that fails, the billionaire retreats and waits. When the corporate gods of war are kinder, he returns with stronger forces, showing no mercy. Shock and awe in waves of stock and cash, too tempting to refuse for shareholders of the vulnerable company. Even white knights – friendly corporate bidders riding to rescue the merger target – turn back to fight another day.

At some point, every weaker company sells or surrenders. At some point, everyone has a price.

The billionaire believes that merger wars in the unbridled free market are closer to raw competition than any other calling. The battle goes to the strongest, the race to the swiftest, the wealth to the wisest. It is Darwinism at hyper-speed, with no time to blink or forgive. Those who fall behind are lame, blind, and dumb – lost sheep at the mercy of wolves.

Unfortunately, there are casualties after each acquisition. People suffer. Employees suffer heart attacks and strokes. Or they file for divorces and bankruptcies, then die of countless causes. Or they get crazy drunk and drive off the highway.

Other deaths are official suicides.

One man locks himself in the garage with the car engine running, spewing carbon monoxide until it sputters and runs out of gas.

A loyal overseas sales manager makes a statement by slashing his stomach *seppuku*-style in his office cubicle. But after the first stab, he curls over in pain and bleeds to death.

Another worker shoots himself with the same kind of handgun that the billionaire carries under his Italian suit. It is a reliable, well-made gun that rarely jams.

When the billionaire hears about the deaths, he tells his secretary to send sympathy cards to the employees' survivors. One grieving family tears up the card and sends it back. Too bad, because the billionaire always includes a $100 check to help defray the funeral costs.

"You'd think they'd be grateful," he says.

"For a $100 gift after the loss of their loved ones?" his secretary says. "To be honest, some probably are offended. I'm sure they would be grateful for flowers, and maybe a few more dollars to start scholarship funds for their kids. They aren't as lucky and blessed as you."

The billionaire glares at her.

"Well praise the Lord and pass the offering basket," he says. "I sweated for those blessings. Every dollar, every cent, every bread crumb. My sympathies to the families, but there is no manna from heaven."

Each year, the billionaire jets to India for gatherings of global executives and investors. At the airport, he declines a private helicopter, instead jumping into an armor-plated sedan for the long drive to a luxury hotel by the sea.

On the way to the hotel, the billionaire catches a glimpse of a vast countryside estate. It is the $2 billion private home of a renowned tycoon and his wife, who hail from more countries than most people can name. Resembling a resort, the property boasts fifty rooms and suites, a small concert hall, a gymnasium and Olympic-size swimming pool, a ballroom and conference rooms, a fleet of cars and trucks, and a helicopter for quick hops to the airport. Local planners stopped at allowing a small runway.

"Is this Mumbai or Versailles?" the billionaire says to himself. "I wouldn't buy that castle at fire-sale prices. I couldn't afford it anyway."

East or West, old money or new, no matter. The billionaire's frugal ways and Spartan lifestyle would have pleased his father.

While some favor estates and vineyards, the billionaire lives in a plain, gray, seven-bedroom house in America. Dubbed "The Compound" by critics, the block-like home and its plain yard lack elegant decor and landscaping, and it commands less than ten million dollars in market value. Its saving grace: it perches on a granite cliff beside the cobalt blue ocean, near a towering steel bridge that spans the harbor strait.

Periodically, the billionaire must host receptions for clients, investors, the media. To fill the bare house, the billionaire's staff hires a furniture-staging firm to bring in sofas and chairs, dining and coffee tables, paintings and pictures – anything to make the home look cozier than a catacomb.

"You don't spend much time here, do you?" a journalist asks the billionaire.

"The office is home and hearth," he says, winking.

During winters on the windswept hill, the billionaire turns off the heater to remind him of the hardships that his ancestors faced. If they built new lives in the pre-industrial frontier, the billionaire can sleep without heat in a sparsely furnished home.

The billionaire's only vehicle, a large Ford truck, sits in a small garage under the house. For once, he heeds the advice of his security team and has the black SUV fitted with steel plates, bulletproof windows, and heavy-duty tires.

Under the garage, he has built a survivor's safe room in case of a huge storm or earthquake. A small escape tunnel leads to a nearby bluff. Outside, security cameras and guard dogs ward off burglars and corporate spies.

The billionaire's house mirrors his austere daily schedule.

Each morning, he arises at 4:59 a.m. sharp – always a minute before 5 a.m., to remind him that time is wasting. His morning regimen in his exercise room keeps him in decent fighting shape for a seventy-five-year-old CEO.

He steps on a treadmill and jogs or walks briskly for twenty minutes. Then he straps himself to a weight-lifting machine for another twenty minutes of sweating.

As he exercises, he watches the business news. Kill two birds with one blast. His favorite shows: the ones that cover the news rapid-fire, bam bam bam, without the numbing commentary by talking heads filling dead airtime.

Fitness classes? That's for yoga teachers, who make good money off white-collar clients. White-collar clients who work for nice companies. Nice companies that create good jobs. Good jobs filled by well-paid employees, who become clients of the yoga teachers. It's the circle of commerce, the journey of worldly goods. Yoga teachers should be grateful for compassionate capitalists such as the billionaire, who values all consuming creatures in the universe. *Namaste* that, he thinks.

The billionaire won't admit it, but he could use a good yoga class to loosen his limbs and strengthen his heart. While exercising a few years ago, he felt faint and nauseous enough to rush to the hospital. His doctor gave him medication, and advised surgery. "Thanks, but no thanks," he told the doctor. "I hear sometimes your patients never wake up."

Any ailment is the last thing on his mind today, as the billionaire hits the two-mile mark and steps off the treadmill. He lifts a few weights, then stretches and towels his sweat.

Workout done, the billionaire heads upstairs for his ten-minute bathroom and bedroom drill. He figures that he has spent three months showering and shaving over his lifetime. An entire fiscal quarter. All of that lost productivity.

Wiping steam off the sink mirror, the billionaire stares at a plain man that few would notice at a social event, if not for his status. A bald scalp with weed-like white hair. A forehead gouged with wrinkles that resemble cracks in dried mud. A sharp, narrow nose fit for a bird of prey. Dark green eyes that would be emerald, if not for the scowling. Taut, shriveled lips, stretched tighter from nonstop grimacing.

The billionaire's genes hail fresh from the fountainhead, a blend of Europe, Russia, Asia, Africa. A scholar friend calls it classical mulatto. Never mind the Mayflower and Plymouth Rock. The billionaire's genes probably stretch back to the dawn of mankind. When the billionaire hears that, he smiles as proudly as tribal leaders hearing the news.

The billionaire rubs his smooth, rounded chin. His large dimples come from his mother's side. Since he has no wife and children, the family lineage might end with him.

All the more reason to dress well, to represent the last of his kin. No jeans and khakis for him. Each workday, without fail, he wears a sharply-pressed, navy blue wool suit. The exact same suit. After each quarter, he tosses the suit and grabs a fresh one. Sustainable wear for CEOs.

Selecting a scarlet tie and a crisp, light-blue shirt, the billionaire quickly ties a full Windsor knot that falls perfectly straight to his belt buckle. He demotes managers who come to work with the easy-to-tie, half-Windsor knots – a sign of lukewarm ambition.

Lastly, the billionaire slips on one of his seven black dress shoes, rotating one for each day of the week. Lined neatly in the closet, the spit-and-polish shoes are spaced three inches apart, to allow the leather to breathe. When those seven shoes wear down, he orders seven more.

After dressing, the billionaire dashes to the kitchen for his ten-minute breakfast. He wolfs down coffee, toast, egg whites, and oatmeal. To save time, he chews while washing and drying the dishes. No cook or housekeeper needed.

By 6 a.m., the billionaire strides to the front door, eager to beat the rush-hour traffic.

Passing an entryway table, he glances at a silver picture frame that holds a wedding portrait of his late father and mother. They gaze at the camera in the perfect tranquility of wedding photos. At the top of the picture frame rests a small, gold-plated cross with the crucified Jesus. The photo and frame are among only a handful of family heirlooms, and likely will vanish after the billionaire's death.

The billionaire's ancestors were not captains of industry in the same class as Carnegie or Rockefeller, Stanford or Huntington. They did not launch banks, railroads, entire industries. No universities bear their names. But they helped to build their state's economic empire, larger than most nations.

Surely, the billionaire thinks, some museum will stage exhibits honoring the state's 20th century business epoch. His family's business era.

"We'd still be riding horse-drawn carriages if it wasn't for us," he says to himself, hopping into his hulking Ford. "How about a little goddamn gratitude?"

There is nothing at home that awaits him, except for his guard dogs and the furniture on lease. So he stays late in his office, nearly every day.

As part of his pay package, the billionaire had the adjacent office converted into a large study with a bed, an executive's bathroom, a kitchenette and bar, and three flat-screen TVs to watch the global news.

For meals, the billionaire usually gobbles down a roast beef or turkey sandwich at his desk, or he enjoys pasta, seafood, or prime rib in the executive dining room down the hall.

His secretary urges him to rest more, to eat food that won't choke his arteries like grease clogging water pipes.

"You grunt a little louder every time you sit down," she says.

The secretary is in her late forties, and at times she resembles a doting mother, the caricature of a television show Mom. In the same way that immigrants learn English by watching TV, she picked up her homemaking style from Martha Stewart and old Betty Crocker cookbooks.

Each day, she brings her lunch to work, with lettuce-lined sandwiches cut into four quarters, or casseroles packed in clear plastic containers. Sometimes, she brings in freshly baked muffins, butter cookies, or See's candies for her officemates, who call her auntie. The secretary's comfort food easily beats the sludge-like cafeteria meals downstairs.

The billionaire never eats in the cafeteria. But sometimes he'll drop by, as if he's one of the regular workers, when he gives the quick building tour to business guests. One day, he spots a new marketing manager at a table, bobbing his head to a Zebra-colored iPod. When the young man isn't on nightly conference calls with his overseas staff, he performs in a dance troupe that fuses hip-hop with classical Indian dance.

"The food here sucks," the young manager says. "Let's drive somewhere tomorrow."

"At least it's cheap," a friend says. "What's up?"

"Jessie J rockin' it," the young manager says. "Ain't about the ba-bling, ba-bling . . . ." [8]

As the billionaire walks by, he hears the young manager tell his friend, "Our CEO is real old, as in real old fart."

The billionaire grins. He goes over to the surprised young manager, and slaps his back.

"This old fart makes more money in one day than you'll make all year," he says. "I thought all you kids wanted to be billionaires so freaking bad anyway. All hail, old farts."

The billionaire isn't offended. The new manager still is in his honeymoon period. He hears that the kid is sharp, a Stanford MBA and business prodigy who understands global markets and cultures better than graybeards like him. They hired him from a flashy media-and-entertainment company after months of courtship, and only after offering him company stock, plus a job and benefits for his domestic partner.

34

To justify the price tag, a hiring manager calls the kid "an avatar of global cool." The billionaire calls him Bhangra Boy. Most of his new hires come from India, China, and Russia – or places he cannot pronounce.

It's hard to convince young talent to come to a company born in the smokestack era. But the billionaire sells the company's global DNA. ("Would you rather sit in a cubicle all day, or travel the world and lead teams into battle? Your choice.") He talks up his rock-solid business and its real revenue, not startup hype. ("We may be old school, but money never gets old, does it?") Nor does it hurt to offer the recruits stock options pegged to their performance and company gains. ("Skin in the game never hurts.")

The young globals remind the billionaire of himself when he had fresh scalp growth. Hungry, ambitious, toiling day and night.

Of course, the young globals weren't born into the billionaire's wealth. Much of the billionaire's early success came from his inheritance and his father's glad-handing, back-slapping business network in New York, London, Hong Kong. But after the head start from Pops, the billionaire earned his standing the old-fashioned way, by the sweat of his rawhide brow.

Reap what you sow, he believes. No time for the faint-hearted. No hope for the frail. It sounds cold, but that's the way of the world.

In the billionaire's realm, there is not even time or room for marriage and the requisite trophy wife.

Some women, he thinks, are like bad debt after an acquisition gone sour. They are more trouble than their net worth. You cannot write them off. You cannot call them goodwill.

Besides, he covets the corporate monastery. No distractions, no demands, no drama. He escorts women to soirees for show and public image, but he never leads them on.

God, there is no shortage of women. And he is the first to admit that he's an old, ugly, single man who happens to be wealthy. If he was dirt poor, not filthy rich, they wouldn't look twice at him.

Money always has been the paramount aphrodisiac. That's no secret. But the billionaire is amazed at how alluring even a peek at his bare assets can be to some women. What if he was a real corporate rock star, a jetsetter with payloads of testosterone gushing through his veins?

His secretary, who looks as good as the money-grubbing rabble and who makes much more sense, does her best to fend off the parade of suitors. But still they come, like birds of sundry feathers.

There are the groupies who sniff money like scavengers smelling carrion. Models who glean gold-digging techniques from legal transcripts of divorce cases. Patrons and heiresses, eager to please at glittery charity events. Stylish, thirty-something careerists willing to bonk their way to the C-Suite. Rich foreigners, skilled at flattering Westerners at embassy dinners.

But no matter how poised and polished the women are at the social game, they salivate when they spot the billionaire from afar. As he nears them, they lean in. Their eyes light up. They touch their hair and moisten their lips. Their faces, made up to meet the faces that they meet, break into wide, bank-breaking smiles.

Like piggish men ogling pretty girls for their looks, even the most good-hearted, altruistic women cannot see past the dollar signs, the billionaire thinks.

Over drinks with another CEO, the billionaire shakes his head and laughs.

"They just want my gold-plated balls," he says.

CHAPTER TWO

The Secretary

"Taking makes me feel like I'm dying. Giving makes me feel like I'm living."

—MITCH ALBOM, AUTHOR.[9]

SILVERWARE CLINKS AS the banquet speaker blathers on. It's long past dessert. Diners fidget and rub their eyes, eager to go home. The secretary excuses herself to visit the restroom.

She weaves through the hotel ballroom when a tall, clean-shaven businessman rises from his seat.

He leans in and grabs the secretary by the crook of her elbow. His grip is strong, digging into her skin and muscle through her suit and blouse. She winces and yanks her arm away.

"I don't mean to interrupt your nap," says the businessman, smelling of cocktails, "but were you planning to take our plates before this weekend? We were done a while ago."

"Excuse me, I don't work here," she says.

"Oh, forgive me, you look like the help."

People turn to stare at them. A few smile and chuckle.

It seems like a minor insult, a social snub by a half-drunk entrepreneur. But the countless indignities, small and large, wear away the secretary, like stomach acid burning a hole in her gut.

At male-dominated business gatherings, many mistake her for a hotel employee. Nothing wrong with hotel workers. But the instant branding, the classifying of her into a genus based on gender, happens too often.

Maybe it's her polite bearing, her solicitous manner, that some perceive as docile. Or her accent on the occasional word, like an off-pitch note in a song. Or her slightly crimped hair, her terracotta skin hue. Her broad nose and rounded cheekbones, the signs of ancestry in a distant, non-Anglo land.

"Inuit," says one executive, admiring her during a reception.

"Pardon me?"

"You're Inuit, an Eskimo," he says, as if appraising a breed at a dog show. "You have aboriginal blood in you."

Nothing wrong with Eskimos, either. But after twenty-five-years in corporate land, the secretary resembles a middle-aged, professional woman who reports to a billionaire.

Her pricy wool and silk jackets and skirts aren't standard hotel staff issue, and she did not buy her Italian leather pumps at the local shopping outlet. Dark brown, softly-curled hair frames her oval face. She wears designer eyeglasses and light makeup.

Coworkers say that she resembles a private-school principal or a courthouse judge. One office mate jokes that she can play a young Sonia Sotomayor in a TV movie of the U.S. Supreme Court justice.

The secretary knows that her kind is a low-ranking caste in the corporate hierarchy. The dearth of women in boardrooms is clear; the low numbers don't lie. In much of the business domain, women still are judged by appearances. We can bear the race and fly into space, she thinks, but we cannot run companies.

Working as an accountant and an office manager after business school, the secretary jumped at the billionaire's job offer nearly twenty years ago. The salary and benefits were good, plus she wanted the chance to learn from a world-class executive and business leader.

The secretary soon found out that it's still a rich man's world. Even though she serves as the billionaire's proxy at meetings and events, many businessmen barely glance at her.

The secretary does not mind the grind at work, the late nights. Nor does she mind the billionaire's biting words and harsh manner. But she does mind the hordes of bankers and lawyers – donned in fine suits, swinging big briefcases – that march past her each day, as if she was an invisible thing.

Despite their disregard, the secretary politely greets the parade of dealmakers to the billionaire's office.

"He'll be with you shortly," she says. "Would you gentlemen like some coffee or tea? Some water?"

Too late. The businessmen – and more careerist women nowadays, she notices – do not hear her. Some interrupt her greeting before she finishes. Others smile in that polite business way, before checking their mobile phones. Still others don't bother with the pretense, ignoring her when they enter the room, and letting associates announce them.

One businessman stomps out of a conference room, almost slamming a mug on the secretary's desk. "We've been up all night vetting this proposal," he says. "Don't you have stronger coffee?"

When she brings them their caffeine fix, they stare at their laptops, reviewing their talking points for their meetings with the man that they hope to emulate. They've worked hard to grab fifteen minutes of face time with the billionaire. Imagine actually doing business with him. The halo would last their entire careers.

When visitors hear the billionaire stroll out to greet them, they flash counterfeit smiles at the secretary. They grin and ooze charm, complimenting her outfit. They chat about the weather, the office décor, the picture of her and her parents.

On the surface, their rude behavior seems only to be poor etiquette. But the secretary knows that their treatment of her – when no one is watching – reflects how they treat

41

everyone, from support staff to senior executives. They measure the value of every exchange, weigh the costs of every hello. To them, some people are golden and worth the effort, while others are tossed out like delivery boxes.

The secretary's instincts regarding business men are dead-on. She sees past the façade. And she wouldn't want some of the billionaire's dodgy partners and investors touching her money, much less companies valued at billions of dollars.

Sometimes, she mentions her observations to the billionaire. He dismisses her concerns as naïve.

"It's business, not a playground for saints and angels," he says, not looking up. "If that kind of behavior offends you, you need a thicker skin."

The secretary learned at a young age about man's cruelty and kindness – twin impulses that seemed to rise from the same deep-rooted source. As a little girl, she had witnessed both.

On many nights in her parents' homeland, the little girl heard the rapid-fire pops and echoes of gunfire in the distance. Or louder, booming shots and explosions nearby that awakened her, screaming and crying. She often ran to her father and mother's bedroom, seeking what she believed to be warmth and safety.

"Don't be afraid," their father said. "Always remember your prayers."

With blood lust and impunity, the men with guns lorded over the families in the little girl's town. If storeowners such as her father and mother did not give money to the armed men, their loved ones were kidnapped and killed. Their bodies were chopped up like pigs and chickens at the marketplace, then piled in fields or lined alongside roads.

Some of the gunmen must have worked at butcher shops or meat-packing plants; the guttings of bodies were too skilled, too precise. The men seemed to cut the corpses with care and reverence, perhaps hoping that God might show them mercy when their time came.

The killers always escaped to the jungle, or back to their respectable lives. The lines blurred among the police and military, the paramilitary and criminal gangs, the corrupt judges and politicians. The little girl's family only knew that they could not hide.

For generations, the family had found solace in their church. They sought refuge from hunger and poverty, escape from earthquakes and hurricanes.

"The church is your sanctuary and your shield," the father told the little girl. "The big angels will protect you. They will watch over you."

Over the months, however, the violence worsened against business owners and anyone with money. Religious leaders, urging the gunmen to cease in God's name, were kidnapped and never found. Women and children were shoved into vehicles that vanished into the countryside.

Telling none of their friends and neighbors, the little girl's family quietly left their homeland for America. They took only some clothes, their wedding rings, and her mother's pearl ring given to her by her mother.

They fled with the help of sanctuary churches run by clergy and parishioners, who endangered their lives by their courageous actions. To cross the border, the little girl's family joined a small church group on a cultural and religious exchange hosted by a church in America.

Men tortured and killed the innocent, but men also provided safe haven and passage for many. The cycles of brutality and goodness were never-ending, like the economic cycles that create poverty and wealth.

In America, there were many blessings for the little girl's family. After meeting with social workers and volunteers, the family settled in a low-income neighborhood of a large city, where the father found work as a restaurant manager, and the mother enrolled in nursing school. A resilient immigrant kid, the little girl adapted quickly, learned English, excelled in school.

But the nightmares did not seem to wane. It was as if the armed men had trailed them to America. Any day, they might grab them in the early-morning hours, toss them into a dark cargo hold with other refugees, and ship them back to their homeland like sacks of rice and grain.

The girl's father always felt a chill whenever he saw people in official uniforms. Police officers. Postal workers.

Even Boy Scout troops. Once, he slammed the door on a deliveryman carrying gifts from their friends back home.

Nearly every day or night, gunfire echoed through their neighborhood. On one Good Friday night, a police helicopter swooped over their apartment building. The loud thumping rattled loose windows and set off car alarms. Searchlights swept across the streets, lighting dark corners. The police warned residents to lock up and stay inside.

When the gunfire sounded close, the father turned off the lights, and rushed the little girl and her mother into the bathroom. As the helicopter circled overhead, they took cover in their cold, white bathtub, holding each other. They would be safe from the bad men, the father told his child.

"Stay down, little angel," he said. "Isn't it fun to lie in the bathtub with no water? We're like little lambs in the manger! It's an adventure!"

The girl's father covered their bodies with his own slight frame. He knew that his flesh would not shield them. Nor could he stop intruders breaking into the family's tiny, moldy apartment. But at least his warm body might make his trembling child and wife feel more secure. Whether they noticed his shaky voice, he did not know.

He was the little girl's protector, her guardian. But he was as frightened as they were, lying in the bathtub, curled into balls like rabbits in a den, praying each night that they heard gunshots and the police helicopters.

The little girl never let it show. But beyond her fear, she sensed her father's helplessness. She always knew when

45

something was wrong. She felt his wavering spirit, despite his best efforts to shield her from the dangers outside, or to make a better living in the new land.

Once, while giving thanks for dinner, her father had apologized for failing his family as a provider. He had dreamed of being an educator or a clergyman, but he could not afford the schooling. Nor was he destined to be wealthy. But he was blessed with the riches of a loving wife and daughter, he told them.

"For where your treasure is," he prayed, "there will your heart be also." *Saint Matthew 6:21.*

The spiritual homilies gave small comfort to the secretary. As she grew older, she began to believe, in her bleakest moments, that the laws of God and man were cruel and capricious, blessing a fortunate few while abandoning many others.

How else to explain the flight of an armed robber's bullet, hurtling through the night air, missing the police chasing him on the street, piercing the drywall of the decaying apartment, striking the little girl's mother near an artery in her neck?

The wound spouted dark, rich blood, and her father could not stop it. Even though he called 911 for help, even though he packed gauze on the wound, even though the police and paramedics raced to their home, the little girl only could shriek helplessly as her mother made odd moaning sounds before dying in the cold, white bathtub.

The mother did not depart in a chariot escorted by angels. She did not gaze soulfully at her daughter, whispering words of wisdom in her dying breaths.

Rather, her face twisted into a grisly visage of pain, a silent scream. Her eyes flared in panic, then turned dull and still, as if she had frozen to death on a slab of ice. If she was thinking of her daughter during those last moments, the little girl would never know.

Early in her life, the secretary learned that there were boundless acts of bravery and brutality in the world. The acts of loving kindness that she learned about while growing up seemed as far away as the stars.

At mid-life, memories and visions converge. The secretary sees the beginning and the end of her days with more clarity than ever.

She recalls the little girl at church, doing what every well-behaved child does during sermons. She sat politely for a while, but soon grew fidgety.

"Daddy, when can we go?"

Her father quieted her, but she kept talking. In her homeland, parishioners looked back at her and smiled. In America, congregation members looked back at her and frowned, then whispered to each other.

Their church in America looked fresh and new, as if springing overnight from the soil. There were stained-glass windows and clean, varnished pews. No one had to share ragged hymn books with torn pages. A boys' choir and organ music, rich and deep, colored the worship hall with celestial tones. *"The rich man at his castle / The poor man at his gate / He made them high and lowly / He ordered their estate."* [10] Ushers passed around velvet offering bags stuffed with crinkly money.

The worshippers were well-dressed and smelled of clean laundry, as if church elders had banned foul odors. The balding fathers wore well-tailored suits and shiny dress shoes. Mothers showed off their white and yellow Easter hats and fancy hairstyles. In Sunday school, the boys sported clip-on ties and freshly-ironed shirts, while the girls donned bright bows and flowery spring dresses.

None of the children talked to the little girl, so she turned inward. She stared in wonder at the gauzy rays of sunlight overhead. Pretending her fingers were crayons, she tried to trace and color their contours. But each time she came close to finishing, the sunrays fluttered away

"This is your home," her father said. "When I'm gone, this is your home."

The little girl did not know why her father called this church her home. She did not feel welcome. They sat in the back, away from well-dressed parishioners. During potlucks and socials, congregation members put on their good Christian faces when clergy were nearby, but ignored the little girl and her father when no ministers were in sight. In Sunday school, the other kids never played with the little girl.

In one class, a boy told her, "You look dirty! You should clean yourself and buy a new dress!"

When the little girl cried, the teacher shushed her. As the boy smirked, the teacher dropped a box of tissues at the girl's feet, and told her to blow her nose and wipe her eyes. "Behave," the teacher said. "In America, we have manners."

That did not discourage her father from staying at the church for most of the girl's childhood. The little girl wanted to find a new Sunday school, but he made her stay until she felt comfortable and had made a few friends, including the boy who had taunted her.

"Do you remember what the pastor told you?" her father said. "Do you remember what he said? Look within for faith, then find it in others."

Over the years, through college and the ceaseless hunt for the perfect job, the secretary leaves old churches and finds new ones. No matter the turmoil in her life, she retreats to houses of worship for respite and renewal. The hymns and homilies comfort her. The words lift her spirit.

Since childhood, the secretary has seen her father sacrifice daily, never asking for anything.

While she works, he takes care of her small, tidy house, and he even cooks for her. He has been humble and generous to a fault.

But one winter night, he shows a rare flash of impatience, insisting that his daughter come home early for dinner. He knows that she is busy, but he tells her that this is important.

They talk over supper. How is her job? he asks. Do your bosses treat you well? Are you proud of your work? I know your mother is very proud of you.

"How are you feeling, Daddy?" the secretary asks. "You're sleeping when I get home, so we never get the chance to talk."

"Oh, don't worry about me," he says.

Her father does not tell her that his health has waned recently. One morning, he fainted on the lawn and slammed his head on the grass. Usually upbeat, he has become angry and impatient over minor things. He never eats full meals, and he cannot read books or the Bible like he used to do. He cannot drive, so he no longer volunteers at church. He is weary of his ailments and his isolation.

He has the growing sense that his time has come to pass, and he often dreams of reuniting with his wife in heaven. She calls to him in his dreams.

"You're safe now, you have a good job," her father says. "Maybe it's time for me to see your mother again."

"Don't be silly," the secretary says. "You have a lot of good years left. You can't leave me yet."

Her father smiles and tells her to close her eyes. He reaches into his coat pocket and pulls out a small object. It is a silver jewelry box, wrapped in a small gold bow. He places the gift in her hands.

The secretary unwraps the bow and opens the little box.

"Oh my God," she says.

It is a pearl ring, her mother's old ring, gleaming under the dim restaurant lights. It is the family's sole heirloom, the only thing of value that they brought from their homeland.

"Your grandmother gave this to your mother before you were born," the father says. "This ring was worth more money than anything. We had suitcases and clothes, but that was nothing. It was not safe to wear the ring. So your mother fastened it to a barrette, and pinned it in her hair to hide it.

"You were too small to remember. We went to the airport with a church group. They took care of our passports, our transportation, everything. Almost everyone had gone through the security lines, when the guards stopped us and the church group leader.

"They took us to a room. They asked questions for a long time. They took you to another room, and a lady asked you questions. They were going to let your mother and you go through, but they wouldn't let me and the church leader go with you. They did not say why.

"Your mother pleaded with them, but they refused to let us go. You were crying. Finally, your mother took the pearl ring and barrette from her hair. She cupped it in her hands, and offered it to the guards. She told them 'Please, please take this. It was my mother's ring.' She did not know if they would arrest her for bribery, and steal the ring anyway. Finally, they took it and let us leave.

"In America, I was angry. We had nothing. We lost many things, but why did we have the pearl taken from us?

51

That ring had seen everything, all of the happy times and the bad times. Every day, I was very angry. It was not only the ring. I could not find good work, I could not provide for my family. For the first time in my life, I lost faith.

"But your mother! For some reason, she always thought that she would get the ring again. She said things would get better for us. I told her to stop being silly. This was not a fairy tale. But she never gave up believing this.

"Months later, the church group in America received a large envelope in the mail. We had no idea what it might be. We tore the envelope and opened it. We could not believe it. It was your mother's ring, still on the barrette! No one had touched it! No one had stolen it!

"There was a note from a military man at the airport. He was there when his soldiers took the ring from your mother. Every Sunday, during Mass with his wife and children, he thought of the pain on your mother's face. Others had suffered more. But he remembered your mother and all of the sorrow caused by his soldiers.

"The military man wrote that they did not like hurting their fellow countrymen, and he promised that one day, it would end. 'I am very sorry for taking your beautiful ring,' he wrote, 'and I humbly ask for your forgiveness.'

"After that, I became more devoted than ever. Your mother was right, wasn't she? She put on the pearl ring that day, and she wore it for the rest of her life, like her mother. Now, it is three generations of women who wear it in our family! It is a pearl for you, little angel. A lodestar from afar! So you will always remember."

The secretary gets up to hug her father.

"Thank you, Daddy, this is beautiful," she says. "I feel blessed."

It is getting late, so her father goes to bed. The secretary sips her tea in the kitchen and looks at the ring, already snug on her finger. She is touched that her father told her the family tale, and that he admitted to his loss and rebirth of faith. The sharing of his memory, however painful, bestowed deeper meaning on the gift.

The father hopes to start a new tradition for his daughter, to pass on to her future daughter. She is alone in America, and she will not return to their ancestral homeland. Before he dies, her father hopes that she will find a husband, a life partner, at the church, and start a family of her own.

If the ring is as precious as her father says it is, then the secretary needs to get a small safe for her jewelry and valuable documents. Out of curiosity, she takes the ring to a jeweler that weekend.

"Well," he says, peering at the ring, "this is well-made, but it's not a natural pearl. A few hundred or a thousand bucks at most, plus sentimental value."

The secretary is disappointed, but it doesn't really matter. All that matters is that she honors her father's gift, that she honors his belief in her.

To the secretary, the ring is a keepsake as valuable as the spirit of a loved one. When bodies pass away, something must live on, she thinks.

That spring, shortly after celebrating his eightieth birthday with his daughter and a few friends from church, her father dies calmly in his sleep.

At the moment of his passing, the secretary awakens to a warm chill. The chill rolls up her spine and across her scalp. She shivers. She knows that she is not dreaming.

She hears her father's voice, calling for her. She hurries to his bedroom, knowing already that he is gone.

Before calling the funeral home, the secretary sits on the bed and says a quick prayer.

She lifts onto her lap her father's light, gaunt body. Cradling his head, she strokes his face, his forehead and cheeks. His mottled skin crinkles at her touch. She runs her fingers through his wavy black hair, then leans over and inhales his scent. She hopes to carve into her mind every trait, every feature, of the man who guided her through life.

"Thank you, Daddy, thank you for everything," she says.

Kissing her father goodbye, she prays once more for his departed soul, before the sorrow overtakes her.

At the secretary's request, the pastor at her new church delivers her father's eulogy.

He tells mourners the biblical parable of the poor widow. It is the secretary's favorite. Her father had told her the tale many times when she was little.

"And Jesus sat against the treasury," the pastor says, "and beheld how the people cast money." *Saint Mark 12:38-44.*

Many who gave to the temple treasury were among the richest and most powerful men in the land.

They showed off their wealth with fancy clothing and possessions. They demanded the finest seats at feasts and in synagogues. They took over the houses of widows who no longer could afford their homes. They prayed in public for show and pretense, not out of real faith.

Then Jesus looked up, the pastor says, and saw a poor widow approach the temple treasury. Her clothes were shabby. She had lost her house. But she still cast into the treasury two copper coins – all that she owned.

The Lord told his disciples that this poor widow had cast more into the temple's treasury than the wealthy worshippers in all of their abundance. She gave everything that she had, all that she had to live on.

The pastor looks up at the mourners filling the pews.

"There are a lot of people in the world like the wealthy men. They fill their lives with so many *things*. Flashy cars, fancy clothes, big mansions. They spend all of their riches on themselves, and in the unusual moments when they do give, it's to impress others.

"The man we are praising today was not a rich man, not a famous man, not a powerful man. But he gave generously of himself over the years, far more than he could afford, far beyond his means.

"What is the value of such a man? He devoted the most precious moments of his life to something greater than his needs, and we cannot ask for more of anyone. Sometimes those with the least, give the most. Sometimes those discounted by society ought to be held in the highest esteem.

"Words are fleeting. But some words ring true, over all of these centuries. 'He who sows sparingly shall reap sparingly, while he who sows bountifully shall reap bountifully.' " *Second Corinthians 9:6.*

The pastor looks toward the secretary.

"Your father," he says, "lived and reaped bountifully, and he will be remembered."

Mourners file slowly past his casket, laying flowers inside. The secretary cannot bear again to see her father's waxen face. The viewing the night before was enough. She stays seated until the funeral ends.

Despite the pastor's words, she cannot find sanctuary from the grieving.

Her mother died nearly forty years ago. But with each sharp noise and distant boom, the secretary relives her violent death as if it had happened the night before. And now, she will relive her father's passing each night in her prayers.

The secretary has asked people to donate to her church, rather than buy flowers. The mourners respond generously, giving $10,000 in her father's name. Even the poorest parishioners give their time and money to the church's food and social programs that her father had supported.

The secretary does not expect a gift from the billionaire. She writes and e-mails his replies to charitable requests, so she knows how he thinks.

His stingy business habits are legendary, and his penny-pinching holiday gifts to workers are an annual joke. While rival companies dole out cash bonuses and honey-baked hams during boom years, the billionaire hands out gift baskets with soda crackers and string cheese from the local wholesale warehouse.

Without the secretary's knowledge, the billionaire has mailed to her church the usual $100 check that he sends to his employees who have lost loved ones.

Her face reddens as she apologizes for her Scrooge-like boss and his shallow pockets.

"Not a problem," her pastor says. "We're grateful for every dollar."

"I don't begrudge him his wealth," she says, "but I don't know why he's so miserly."

"People give for different reasons. Sometimes for recognition, or to please others. The more cynical think they can buy their way into God's graces. Few give purely for the sake of giving, out of selflessness. Your boss may not be ready, and that's fine. Every man gives as he is able."

"Why do those who have so much, seem to care so little?"

"So we're grateful," the pastor says, "when we see true acts of generosity."

When the secretary returns to work, the billionaire does not apologize for missing the memorial service, a ten-minute drive from the office.

He says only that his calls to Beijing and Bangalore ran long and late the night of the funeral.

"Yes," the secretary says, "I know you've been busy."

"I'm sorry for your loss," he mutters. "Listen, get some flowers for your father. Call the florist and order a $100 bouquet – no, make it $200 – for his gravestone, at the company's expense. Make sure our name stays on it, so people know where it came from. Sound good?"

"Yes, I'll make sure the company name is on the flowers," she says.

The billionaire notices his secretary's new scarf and dress that she bought for her father's funeral. He stares at her and frowns.

"Try silk or wool next time," he says. "Synthetic blends look cheap in the sun."

Then he eyes her new ring. He leans in to peer at it.

"Is that a Mikimoto, or a fake?" he says. "The powder and polish on good imitation pearls can look like the real thing. It's not real, is it?"

"You're right, it's not a cultured pearl. It was a gift from my father, before he passed."

"Not bad for a glass bead. You know it's just a polished glass bead, right? Did he get it from the jewelry mart, that wholesale place?"

"I don't know," the secretary says.

Angered by the billionaire's words, the secretary's coworkers sit in silence. Even senior executives say nothing, only peeking from their offices, then closing their doors.

A nearby marketing executive, a former professional athlete who still competes on weekends, hears the talking and steps out of her office. She is the only executive to speak up.

"Considering her father just died," she says, "a little show of sympathy would be appropriate. You act as if she's some faceless outsourcing hire, much less your office manager for as long as you can remember."

The billionaire stares at his executive.

"If I were you," he says, "I'd worry less about my secretary, and more about landing that World Cup deal. Especially after you screwed up the Olympics. You're a global marketing executive who can't market and who hasn't gone global. What good are you?"

The marketing executive glares so hard at the billionaire that it looks as if she might charge down the hall at him.

The support staff quietly cheers the outspoken executive. They hope that she confronts the billionaire, so he'll back down like all office bullies.

But the executive shakes her head, and returns to her office.

The secretary gets up, grabs her purse, and hurries to the women's restroom. Standing in a bathroom stall, she stifles her sobs in tissues and toilet paper.

Another secretary checks on her. "Honey, you okay?" she asks.

"Yes, I'm fine," the secretary says, drying her eyes. "Thanks for asking."

She is not fine. The humiliation swamps her, as if someone has flung raw sewage at her face and her dress. It stings to the touch and blisters her skin. The hurt feels like a scaly, living thing, coiling and filling her insides, pressing against her heart and lungs.

Her head throbs. Greenish-yellow bile rises in her body. She retches and vomits into the toilet, then flushes to get rid of the smell.

In a rare outburst, the secretary curses and spews hatred at the billionaire. She loathes him as much as she hated the soldiers who hurt her mother. Such an ugly, ungodly man. She pictures his craggy, sneering, serpent-like face. She wants to claw him until he bleeds, until his skin tears.

She despises the billionaire for his greed, his callousness, his unfeeling words. He possesses the gifts to help others, yet he hoards those gifts, and he cannot see others in deep pain and suffering.

Like the maintenance man and his blood-red sign on the billionaire's door, the secretary hopes that her boss suffers more than the pain he has inflicted on his staff. *Burning for burning, wound for wound.*

She hopes that the billionaire is plagued by terrible accidents and ailments: A car crash that snaps his vertebrae, paralyzing him. Killer cancer cells that course through his body. A stroke that leaves him helpless and drooling on the floor.

Thou shalt condemn. Her sweet viciousness pleases her, makes her feel potent and commanding, if only for a few passing moments.

"Sure you're alright?" her coworker asks again. "Don't worry about that creep. He'll get his one day. Honey, if you need anything, let us know."

"Thank you, I'll be right out."

At the sink, the secretary wipes her face and rinses out the bile. Over the past month, she has cried more than she has cried in decades. She brushes her hair, puts on fresh lipstick and eye makeup.

The restroom door opens and two coworkers enter, complaining about rush-hour traffic.

She smiles a polite business smile at them, and heads back to her desk.

At home a few weeks later, the secretary turns off her computer and sighs. It is nearly midnight. She takes off her glasses and rubs her eyes.

She volunteers as her church's treasurer and accountant, but she cannot concentrate on anything since her father's death.

Tomorrow, she needs to finish the church's taxes, and then meet the billionaire and a CEO from Sao Paulo for lunch. The secretary takes notes during the billionaire's meetings, but she also studies the chemistry between the billionaire and potential partners in corporate marriage.

Soft music flows through her living room. Mournful notes, transcendent chords, songs of supplication. The local jazz and indie radio station plays Leonard Cohen: *"Ring the bells that still can ring, forget your perfect offering . . . ."* [11]

Head nodding, the secretary falls asleep on the sofa. She drops her mug, spilling cold tea on the couch and a pile of funeral programs.

Since her father's passing, the secretary has been troubled by visions nearly every night. Most are full of dim shapes and shadows that she barely can recall when she awakens.

But one lucid dream haunts her.

The secretary stands alone in the small kitchen of her small house, in the late-afternoon light.

She leans over the sink, cupping water in her hands. A breath of warm wind fills the kitchen, compelling her to move through the dining room, the living room, the hallway.

She drifts into the spare bedroom where her father spent his last months. She lies in his bed, hoping that he'll appear. She makes the bed, folds his clothes, puts them in the dresser. She goes through his belongings in the closet, and saves a few keepsakes.

Tattered wedding photographs that friends mailed from the old country. A dusty collection of record albums, including Broadway show tunes that he loved. An old Bible marked with dozens of fiercely scrawled notes.

A fervent reader, the father had circled many words and passages in ink. As the secretary turns the pages, the ink turns blood red like stigmata.

One verse that her father had starred was Ecclesiastes 3:21: *"Who knoweth the spirit of man that goeth upward?" Another read: "Curse not the king . . . and curse not the rich . . . For a bird of the air shall carry the voice, and that which hath wings shall tell the matter."* Ecclesiastes 10:20.

Shivering, the secretary senses a figure standing across the room. She rubs her eyes and strains to look. As if peering through white gauze, she sees the contour of her father.

She sees his face. He smiles at her, and hugs her. He clasps her tiny hands.

They step back through the hallway, gaze into other rooms, walk to the kitchen. He straightens her bow and pats her on the head. How was school today, young lady? Did you have fun? What did you learn in class?

63

Before she can answer, her father starts to fade away. No, not now, it's too soon, she pleads. She longs to talk to him, to hear him again, but she cannot speak or move. His voice grows faint.

Do you remember, little angel, what we learned in church, the most precious lessons, the most beautiful lessons of all, judge not and ye shall not be judged, forgive and ye shall be forgiven, please remember my angel, bless you little angel, I love you little girl he says, before fading away.

No, Daddy, come back, please come back.

The secretary never believed in spirits, real spirits, until now.

Her father's visitation haunts her for weeks.

She senses his presence when she awakens each morning, when she falls asleep each night.

At times, she sees his visage. Other times, only his voice or his scent linger.

She silently mouths his words as she drives to work, and as she drives home.

While cooking dinner or checking e-mail, she abruptly bursts into tears.

She thinks she is going crazy.

Then, as swiftly as it appeared, her father's presence vanishes.

Work is a black hole. Late one night after dinner, the secretary returns to the office to get some files for the weekend.

"Evening, ma'am," says the young guard with tattoos.

"Hello there, working the swing shift now, eh?"

"Just for this month. I have training all day, so I'm working nights."

"Well, I hear you're a pretty sharp young man. You'll be running corporate security any day now."

"Thank you, ma'am. I highly doubt it, but I'll take the compliment."

The office is empty except for the billionaire, who stays all night to make long calls to Asia and Europe. The talks last to the early morning, often ending in harsh words between partners. When he is not on the phone, the billionaire mutters to himself, slamming his palms on his desk, cursing at ghosts.

On this night, the secretary peers down the hallway into the billionaire's office, and sees an odd sight.

The billionaire stands motionless, his head down. Occasionally, he lifts his face upward, his eyes closed. His voice is faint. She can barely hear his words. But he seems to be practicing a speech of some sort.

He is paying tribute to someone, honoring someone. He speaks of the deceased in reverent tones, telling the man's life story, reciting his favorite biblical verses and lessons.

At times, the billionaire speaks with passion and conviction. At other times, his words wander. He clears his throat. His voice cracks. He sobs briefly, then wipes the tears.

The secretary peers into the billionaire's office. His bookcase's locked doors are wide open, and he has strewn several rare editions on his desk. She has never seen him touch the books, and he has given firm orders to the janitors not to clean the bookcase.

She is startled to see one book cracked open, its frail spine flattened. Like a college student cramming for finals, the billionaire has marked and underlined several verses in fresh ink. One reads: "The good of grace is in exact proportion to the ardor of love that opens to receive it."[12]

The secretary does not know of any speeches or memorial services on the billionaire's schedule. He has no close family or other loved ones. His parents died long ago, and he never mentions them.

She listens more closely, and smiles. The billionaire is reciting the eulogy that he gave at his father's funeral, a decade ago to the day.

She recalls the service, a small gathering at a cemetery chapel. Given the stature of the billionaire's father, some had expected a large public mass at the French-Gothic cathedral downtown, near the waterfront. But the billionaire's father disliked fancy ceremonies, and he had requested a simple, private service. The father also had requested that only his son read the eulogy.

The billionaire honors his father's wishes and more, reciting the eulogy each anniversary of his death. He also recites his mother's eulogy, read by a minister when the billionaire was a child. He imagines that his parents stand beside him, smiling proudly at their boy.

The eulogies are hard for the billionaire to finish without breaking down. But tonight he feels a surge of inspiration, as if a muse or a guardian is guiding him.

"I can build new businesses, buy and sell companies, from dawn to dusk," the billionaire says. "But my father, a businessman blessed with so much heart and soul . . . He could build a family. He could build a home."

Not wanting to disturb the billionaire, the secretary quietly grabs her files and slips out a side door.

Maybe she is wrong about the billionaire. Like everyone, the billionaire needs solace and sanctuary, an escape from the endless demands of life. And given his standing, his demands must multiply a hundred-fold, a thousand-fold.

Has she been too harsh in damning the man? Who was she to judge? Who was she to condemn? The desire to hate and the desire to forgive seem to be twin impulses, arising from the same source.

The secretary regrets her show of emotion in the office. Even given the billionaire's cold words and actions, her actions were spiteful and malicious. She had let her bitterness consume her, and she vows to never again wish suffering upon another person.

Many in corporate land blindly parrot others. Speaking up and challenging authority have political costs, and countless wage slaves have been fired for less.

The secretary knows how far she can push the billionaire. But it's always a delicate dance. Some days, he'll snap at her, even reprimand her. Other days, he treats her decently. So one day, she marshals her facts and says something that blasts like a bullet past the billionaire's head.

"Do you have a moment?"

"What, for God's sake?"

"I think there's a coup developing in the boardroom."

Taken aback, the billionaire perks up and pays rapt attention. He leans forward in his chair to listen to her.

She did not want to mention it until she was certain. But in recent weeks, it has become clear to her that a band of disgruntled dissident directors has been scheming privately over the fate of the company.

Unnoticed by them, the secretary has overhead snippets of their talk during board breaks and private meetings. She has read several of their e-mails that do not disclose details, but allude to strategic change and a new course for the company. She has quietly lunched with other support staffers, who are privy to more precious information than Wall Street analysts.

The secretary hands the billionaire printouts of the e-mails. He reads the notes, and glares down the hall at the directors' empty offices.

The billionaire confides to his secretary that he reluctantly had invited the directors to join the board decades ago, only to honor the wishes of his parents, who wanted to thank the men who had bankrolled the company. A few of the directors had died since then, so the billionaire felt obligated to hire their heirs, who were as brainless as their fat-cat fathers.

"My folks were grateful to them for their financial backing early on," the billionaire says. "But gratitude only goes so far."

The directors clearly are not suited to oversee a company. They are figureheads long past their primes. They pad their pay packages with perks, from pumped-up pension plans to personal use of the corporate plane. Rather than find the best business partners, they engage in self-dealing and side deals. They cannot audit their own tax returns, much less monitor a *Fortune 500* company. They are paper tigers, not watchdogs.

And now, they are conspiring to betray the man who welcomed them to the board long ago. Who has saved their wrinkled hides in many battles. Who has made them richer, despite their dearth of business chops. Who has shown them much more respect than they deserve.

"To be honest, they put on a good show for you, to win you over," the secretary says. "But they act very differently when you're not around."

The billionaire grins and looks at her, as if seeing her for the first time.

"Are you saying I shouldn't trust the two-faced, brown-nosing bastards?"

CHAPTER THREE

Crossroads

"Wavering between the profit and the loss
In this brief transit where the dreams cross . . . ."

— T.S. ELIOT, "ASH WEDNESDAY"[13]

WALKING TO HIS office downtown, the billionaire notices a man in a dark suit tailing him. He spots the man as they stride past a hotel's glass entrance.

The billionaire keeps walking. As he passes a glass office door, he looks again. The man still is there, trying to blend into the workday crowd.

Instead of heading to his office to meet his advisors, the billionaire stays on the main street, packed with people during lunch hour. He picks up his pace. Cold ocean gusts rip between the high-rise buildings.

The billionaire looks again. The man ducks into the crowd. This time, he studies his pursuer's features, to describe him to the police. Tall, gaunt, in his sixties or older with thin white hair. Wearing a suit, so he fits in the financial district. The man's sharp eyes and sure posture peg him as a retired cop or military officer, or a corporate spook who needs to work on his surveillance.

The billionaire wishes that he had taken security's advice and hired a bodyguard. He reaches under his coat to unclip his holster and ready his handgun, just in case. The man does the same. He carries a firearm in his holster.

"Watch out! That man!" the billionaire shouts. "Call the police!"

People flinch and jerk their heads around, as if they have heard a truck backfire. Others think he is a street person and walk around him.

Oh, for Christ's sake, the billionaire mutters. What an idiot. It dawns on him that the man in the glass is his own reflection. My God, what the hell is wrong with him? He has been paranoid ever since the janitor torched his office. The wooden sign and condemnation nailed to his office door have cut him more deeply than he admits.

He feels like a fussy old fool, doddering around downtown. He has become the old nowhere man that pedestrians squeeze past on the sidewalk.

Two police officers on bicycles look at him for a moment, then pedal past. Someone had called 911. But they had reported his odd behavior, not an imaginary gunman running wild on the streets.

A young man in a button-down shirt and jeans looks at the billionaire.

"You all right there, graybeard?" he asks.

"Yeah, I'm fine. Bad morning. Time to look for a new job."

"I hear you. Been there, done that."

"I'm sure you have, son."

Jesus, how embarrassing. Luckily, the young man and others did not recognize the billionaire from the small, old photo of him and his father in the *Forbes* article.

Year by year, the billionaire more closely resembles his father in his late years. Slender, hunched over, almost skeletal. Deep furrows in his face and neck. A falcon-like visage and guarded eyes.

The billionaire may have looked like his father's successor as CEO of the family's business dynasty. But the son seemed fated for other callings.

As a youth, he had little desire to follow his father into business. Spending his summers working for his father seemed to foreshadow a dull and dismal career. The boy could not imagine spending his entire lifetime running the company.

In college, he studied economics to please his father, but he pursued literature with Dionysian abandon. He devoured Keats and Kerouac, not Keynes and Samuelson. During Sunday dinners with his father, he cited his seminars and research papers – not the mind-blowing rock festivals, the weeklong benders to Henry Miller's Big Sur, the acid-filled road trips to lower Baja before commercial developers showed up. When his studies got rough, it was nothing that some hash oil and free love couldn't fix.

His father may have preordained his son's destiny, but the son rebelled. After one argument over dinner, the son stormed out of the family house in their well-heeled neighborhood and ran to his car. As neighbors peered through windows, the husky father grabbed his full-grown son in a bear hug, then carried the boy back inside.

"Don't ever do that again," he warned.

Decades later, the billionaire still can feel his old man wrap him up like a Greco-Roman wrestler. Enraged at the time, he smiles now and blinks hard to fend off the regret.

The billionaire calls his secretary to push back his meeting with his advisors. If they want his business, they can wait another hour or two.

He turns off his mobile phone and strolls toward the harbor and bay. Nearly every street claims a memory.

Hunting for school clothes and a new baseball mitt with his folks. Eating burgers and fries at shiny lunch counters. Gazing at harbor lights with his girlfriend, behind a fogged-up windshield. Sealing his first business deal at the same hotel where his grandparents signed the legal papers to buy their store a century ago.

During one year of record profits, the billionaire reluctantly hosted a Christmas office party at a stately waterfront building boasting twin bell towers and an arched arcade. His secretary, showing her sound judgment and uncanny feel for her colleagues, had insisted on the site.

The secretary, by far, has been the best assistant hired by the billionaire since he took over the company. She has natural business instincts, often spotting trends and partnerships that the billionaire misses. She convinced him that U.S.-born business partners with immigrant investors and managers are the best of both worlds, with clout and contacts in America and abroad. Or those Canadian and Mexican firms that originally were the billionaire's business allies. She warned that they weren't bluffing, that they would cut deals in China and Russia if the billionaire didn't meet them halfway. She was right.

And given her insights into company politics, she has saved him from embarrassment more than once in the boardroom. Hell, she probably will save him from losing the company to the disgruntled directors plotting his demise.

The billionaire sensed long ago that his secretary was as clever and capable as his higher-ranking executives. But he was too archaic, too narcissistic, to admit it. If he cannot trust her, he cannot trust anyone.

Considering her loyalty and dependability, the billionaire should have shown more gratitude and gone to her father's funeral. Hell, he thinks, everyone has lost loved ones. Everyone grieves. Life is unfair, and survivors move on. But he still should have shown her more empathy in her time of need.

As the billionaire nears the waterfront, old sights and sounds surge into his head, as if a gateway has opened. Sunlight limns the harbor. The wind grows stronger. A light fog spills in, eclipsing half of the sky.

He walks past long-vacant piers, now under construction. On one pier, he spots a rundown burger joint that once boasted the best burgers and hot dogs in town. He and his father ate lunch there before ballgames at the nearby stadium.

Once, they saw a legendary ballplayer chowing down while fans crowded around. The Hall of Famer held court for an hour, signing autographs, telling stories, buying drinks on his dime.

"That's a class act," the billionaire's father had said. "He knows money and fame aren't the keys to the kingdom. You know, everyone learns that eventually. Hotshot athletes and executives. British royalty and Roman emperors. Remember King Solomon? Sad thing is they realize it with hardly any time left to make amends."

So long ago. The billionaire would trade his wealth for a year of walks along the water with his father. He wishes that his father could advise him now, when his biggest challenge is facing his troubled reflection in a glass door.

The billionaire buys coffee and a jumbo hot dog. He drowns the juicy hot dog in catsup and spicy brown mustard, and then sits on a bench in the sun.

Runners and bicyclists, looking like catalogue models, race past him. Tourists stop to study guidebooks. Business people glance at the billionaire, then nod and smile in recognition.

Seabirds swoop in to swipe his food. Tearing a chunk of bread, the billionaire fakes a throw, and the birds fly madly at nothing. He tosses the rest of his hot dog bun into the water and the birds go wild. Ravenous, they flock back to the billionaire. Kicking at the birds, the billionaire spills mustard on his silk tie. He laughs and dabs the tie with napkins, but only smears the mustard more.

Far across the bay, the billionaire admires the port cranes rising against the skyline. Closer, he counts, like a schoolboy, the wooden and concrete piers jutting far into the water.

One of the concrete piers is home to a vintage, firefighting tugboat. As a kid, the billionaire loved to watch that boat. He cannot believe that it still is berthed there. Little remains of the old waterfront, and the tugboat is a historical icon. Over its lifetime, the vessel must have rescued hundreds of boaters and children and suicidal people from the frigid harbor waters.

Recently, the billionaire saw the fireboat bring ashore a homeless person who had jumped from the bridge. A shirtless, gray-bearded man lay in a gurney, wrapped in a blanket, an oxygen mask strapped to his face. Blood seeped from his nose and ears. "Hang in there, pal," a firemen said. "We'll get you to a hospital." As the billionaire moved closer to stare at the scene, a fireman shoved him aside and scolded him. "Can you stand back, Ebenezer?" he said. "You ever hear that the last shall enter first?"

The billionaire sighs and rubs his neck. He could have called the fire chief or the port commissioner and had the fireman suspended or let go, union be damned.

But who is he to condemn the firefighter? In a world of poseurs and pretenders, the fireman is the authentic deal, a real rescuer, a guardian. Any man who risks his life to save others carries a heroic streak and a moral authority that the billionaire never had.

On his most danger-filled days, the billionaire risks capital.

Finishing his coffee, the billionaire gets up to leave. The lunch crowd thins, and the seabirds find other benefactors.

The billionaire turns and sees a rancid-smelling man in a frayed baseball cap, hobbling down the walkway. Breakneck bicyclists swerve around him. One yells at the street person to get out of the way.

The street person ignores the bicyclist. But he sees the billionaire, and he shuffles toward him. He winks his crusty eyes. His lips are cracked and shrunken. White skin flakes cover his face. His calloused hands touch the billionaire.

"I know you got a dollar for me, boss," the street person says. "Make a poor man happy."

The billionaire pats the man's shoulder and hands him a $100 bill.

"Buy some real food and a new baseball cap," he says. "Don't spend it all at once."

Speechless, the street person stares at the money, rubbing it between his fingers.

Who would have thought it, the billionaire muses. He used to scoff at the old TV show with the mystery millionaire, doling out cash to strangers. And now, at the dusk of his life, he is doing it with a feeling resembling joy.

Far across the harbor, a cargo ship crawls toward the strait and the ocean. The ship – a steel behemoth the length of three football fields – looks like a model boat, a child's plaything, against the horizon.

On the surface, the city seems like a toy city, a wonderland. The billionaire can hold the ships and sailboats in the palms of his hands. Like a child hoping to fly home, the billionaire lifts his arms skyward. Raising his fingers, he traces the big buildings, the pretty clouds, his father's world.

The billionaire can hear his father's deep voice, feel his firm and calloused grip, from half-a-century ago.

The day that the billionaire earned his college degree, he did not celebrate on graduation night. While his classmates partied until dawn, he went straight to work. His father marched him to his office building to start his long-awaited corporate apprenticeship. The son sulked and fumed.

"I didn't raise my son to be some drunken clown like your pals," his father said. "Ten years from now, they'll be changing your car oil while you're signing their paychecks."

During his boy's first week at work, his father made him mop every floor and scrub every bathroom in the building, resting only on Sunday. After his son complained that he wasn't born to do this, the father told the janitors to take off the next day. The boy would do their work.

During the second week, the son washed dishes in the company cafeteria. He complained that he should be learning the company's finances, not cleaning the kitchen. The father told two of the kitchen staffers to take off the next day, while his son covered for them.

In the third week, the son worked as a front-desk receptionist, answering phones and greeting visitors. He complained that it was women's work. The father gave the regular receptionist the week off, and he made his son perform her job.

During the fourth week, the son washed and waxed every car in the company fleet, finishing past midnight in the parking garage. He complained that his hands and feet were bloody and blistered.

"This is bullshit," the son said. "How does this help me run the company? You've already decided that I'm gonna take over. So why make me jump through all these hoops?"

The father asked his son to come into his office. He closed the door, and they sat down.

"Son, I'm only telling you this once," he said. "You need to shut the hell up, or get the hell out."

No more playing around, the father said. The son had a simple choice: He could act like a man. Or he could slink away and drown in booze like his buddies, for all the father cared.

The son had to learn the business with the right respect and gratitude, with appreciation for his blessings – or he would lose his inheritance, all of it, with his father's simple signing of legal documents.

The son looked blankly at his father. He didn't believe the threat. The man who stood there was not a lord of industry passing harsh judgment on others. He was the father who said grace each night at the dinner table, who tucked him into bed when he was a little boy.

The son shrugged his shoulders.

"You wouldn't do that," the son said. "After Mom died, you never remarried, so I'm your only surviving heir. I'm the only family member who can take over the business. Unless you've got a mistress and some kids on the side."

Like dry brushwood bursting aflame, the father shot a fierce glare across the room that chilled his son. The glower pierced the boy's chest like a spear.

His father slammed his fists into the steel gray desk, startling employees down the hall. He grabbed a metal folding chair and flung it across the office, nearly hitting his boy. The chair struck the door, and clanged to the floor. The son smirked and said nothing.

"Wipe that smug look off your face, dammit," the father said. "I swear I'll pick you up like that chair and toss you on the street. I'll throw you out with only one lousy paycheck, if you can't even mop your own office and bathroom. You're not gonna live like a sloth off my hard-earned money. No offspring of mine is gonna do that."

The boy's smirk vanished. Rarely had the son seen his father so angry. He tried to appear tough, but he looked pale and scared. His legs shook.

The father shook his head. "What am I gonna do with this boy," he said under his breath. He leaned back in his chair.

"Sometimes you've got shit for brains," he said. "I know you don't care about any of this now. But I swear you'll feel all tore up long after I'm gone. It's gonna hit you like a hammer."

The father wiped his forehead with his handkerchief, then sighed. His face softened.

"I've told you this, son," he said. "I never remarried because I wanted to devote my time to building our business. And because, in truth, no other woman could measure up to your mother. She married me for the right reasons, long before the money and business took off.

"I wish you had known your mother, when you were growing up. You don't remember a thing, do you?

"She almost died giving birth to you. She labored all day and night, and the next day and night. But the umbilical cord had wrapped tight around your body, so you couldn't move down her birth canal. Your little heart kept getting weaker. But your mother wouldn't let them cut her open. She wanted her baby to come into the world as God had intended.

"Finally the doctor said he had to put her to sleep for surgery. Your mother started crying and pleading with him.

'Can we wait a little longer?' she said. The doctor said he was sorry, but he couldn't risk losing your mother and you.

"You must have heard them talking, son, because you started moving that very second. Somehow, your mother and you managed to wiggle and push you out of there. You slid right out, like a yearling or a little lamb. 'Took your sweet time, didn't you?' the doctor said.

"I cried like a baby. Your mother was crying too. She was bleeding real bad, so they rushed her to the emergency room. She didn't get to hold you and feed you until a week later. She always thought that was a bad sign, a bad omen.

"I told your mother it was a good omen that both of you survived. We were lucky. The pastor called you a blessing. All babies are blessed, but he said you were special. You and your mother could have died that day. At least you got to know her a bit, when you were a little boy.

"Your mother would have been proud to see you get that college degree, then go to work. She said if you didn't want to take over the business, you could become a preacher, a doctor, a teacher. How you would make your living didn't matter to her, any more than my money mattered to her.

"But before she died, she made me promise that I would teach you to fend for yourself. She quoted scriptures: 'And an idle soul shall suffer hunger.' *Proverbs 19:15.* And once you knew how to take care of yourself, you could care for others, like a shepherd tending his flock.

"Your mother said that nothing would make her prouder than to see her boy grow up and walk into a room, upright and with integrity of heart, like her grandfather, her father, and her husband. Nothing would make her prouder."

The father looked at his son's bloodshot eyes.

"Don't mean to be so harsh. I just want you to be grateful for what you've got. A lot of people in the world have real serious hardships, but you've been blessed.

"It doesn't come free, either. You've got to be smart enough to know that we're all awfully weak and lame in the eyes of our Maker. And we've got our whole damn lives to prove otherwise."

The wind blows hard off the bay, making the billionaire blink and tear up. Enough sob-sister nostalgia and fifty-year-old memories. He wipes his wet, salty cheeks.

It's getting late, so the billionaire walks back to the financial district. He still has to meet with his advisors, to discuss what to do with his money. The traffic worsens. Cars race through red lights, nearly hitting bicyclists. Rumbling trucks and buses cut off pedestrians.

Near his office, the billionaire passes a rickety shoeshine stand that belongs in an earlier era. He has passed it hundreds of times. But this day, something compels him to turn back.

The elderly shoeshine man is a dried husk of a man who has spent much of his life sitting, hunched over. He has bent down for so long that his joints nearly have fused into that posture. He moves slowly, and he senses the shadows of customers as they approach him. He barely looks up at the faceless suits, reading their newspapers.

"Help you today, sir?" the shoeshine man asks.

"Just a quick shine," the billionaire says. "I see you every day, but I never stop. Are you the owner?"

"Yup, this stand has been in the family for seventy-five years. My father had it since World War II. Most of his customers were businessmen and military men."

"That's a lot of shoes to shine."

"Over two million, but who's counting? Like Micky D's selling burgers."

"You must do well here."

"Naw, business is hard. Costs keep going up, but gotta keep my prices down."

"Tips must be good."

"Nope, business people are tight with their coins. You know who are the best tippers? Ballplayers staying at the hotel over there! They're pretty generous after they win a big game. One time the Yankees were in town, and what's his name, the World Series hero, gave me $20. He said a good shine makes you feel like a king, like a million bucks."

"Well," the billionaire says, "you probably won't remember because you were a kid, but your father shined my old man's shoes almost every week, for God knows how many years. My father said he learned how to shine from watching him."

"No kidding! Ain't that something."

"You probably won't remember this, either. But a long time ago, you gave me and my buddies some great shines the day of our high-school prom, when we were dumb-ass kids."

The shoeshine man cranes his neck to peer at the billionaire.

"Why I remember you," he says. "Sure I do. Your father owned that store downtown, right?"

"Yup, around World War II, like your Pops."

"I remember now. You look like him. You and your baseball buddies wanted a nice shine before your big dance. It looked like the whole team. You boys ran off without paying. You were laughing like it was a big joke, but that was a lot of money back then. My Daddy said 'Boys will be boys.' I said, 'A thief's a thief.' "

"Christ, I'm sorry. I had completely forgotten about that. I'm awfully sorry. We were stupid kids. We didn't know what we were doing. I know it's a lifetime too late, but how can I make up for it?"

"Oh, don't worry about it. It's nothin'. Like you said, you were dumb kids. I forgive you, my son."

"Are you a priest or a businessman? Look, I insist. Let this poor boy do something for you."

"If you're poor, then I'm King Tut."

The billionaire laughs. He hops off the stand and pulls the shoeshine-stand owner into his seat.

"Come on, get up here. Take a break."

"You done this before, poor boy?"

"Every Sunday, my whole life. My Daddy taught me."

"That makes you a pro."

The billionaire smiles and grabs a brush. He scrapes the dirt and grime from the proprietor's worn shoes, and picks out dirt clots from the sole.

"Cream or wax?"

"Both, baby, if you wanna do it right. Ain't particular about much, 'cept my shine."

The billionaire grabs a cloth and applies the polish to the proprietor's shoes. He spreads it gently on the shoe leather in a smooth, rounded motion. Taking his time, he strokes and brushes and polishes the shoes, as if he was hand-waxing a fine car. He lets the shoes dry for a few minutes, then applies more polish and buffs again.

"May I?" the billionaire asks.

"Don't mind if you do."

The billionaire drapes the cloth over his shoulder and grabs a horsehair brush. He spits on one of the proprietor's shoes, spits on the other. Ignoring his aching bones, he buffs the shoes over and over. Grabbing the cloth with both hands, he shines the shoes rapid-fire, back and forth, to a high, proud gloss that gleams in the afternoon sun.

"How's it look, sir?" the billionaire says.

"Not bad, not bad at all," says the shoeshine man, his eyes reddening. "Best shine since my Daddy. Thank you, young man."

"Young man? My knees are killing me. I can hardly stand up."

"You know, no customer's ever done that for me, ever. Grateful to you. Your shine's on the house."

The billionaire thanks the shoeshine-stand owner. As he gets up to leave, he hands the proprietor a wad of $100 bills.

"What's this?"

"You aren't blind, pal. It's a thousand bucks, give or take a hundred."

"Come on, man, you joking? What's this for?"

"I stiffed you and your Daddy when I was a kid. This is the tip that my buddies and I should have given you. Plus interest."

The billionaire is seventy-five going on perpetuity.

Insurers calculate that he'll die any day, while family genes ordain that he'll live into his nineties. Does God play the odds on any of this?

Back at his office, the billionaire tells his attorneys to update his will and other documents. He has no close family, but he still must dole out a lifetime of assets.

He also wants to make sure that his assets stay safe. The world is a dangerous place for the moneyed class.

"If war breaks out," he says, "I'm target practice."

One risk consultant's report for the billionaire sketches many potential global scenarios for this century, including nuclear warfare, climate catastrophes, and riots over food and water. Lovely, the billionaire thinks.

To guard against a financial meltdown, the billionaire spreads his money in many places besides his hidden vaults of gold: Conservative bluechip stocks. Government bonds in stable countries. Tax shelters and offshore accounts. Real estate in emerging countries. Chinese art that only will rise in value. Even his home, where he hides cash under his survival room.

The billionaire also wants to squeeze more from his stock-related pay. In reporting his pay to regulators, he wants his company to use a little-known accounting move that could greatly boost the value of his holdings. The accounting trick is not illegal, although some call it "questionable."

For the billionaire, it is a moderately risky gamble involving paper wealth and boiler-plate accounting rules. He has risked much more over the years. Still, his attorneys and accountants advise against the move.

"To our knowledge, it's not criminal," says an older attorney. "But it's new ground. Unfortunately, there's little or no guidance. "

The older attorney pauses.

"You probably can cash in another $50 million or so this year," he says. "You don't really need it, though. You'll already get $100 million, $110 million, in stock-related compensation by reporting it the usual way.

"Why take chances and raise raise red flags? Why piss off regulators and prosecutors? They love nailing the hides of CEOs like you to the wall. They love staging press conferences and 'perp walks' for the media. One big case can make their careers. It's not worth the risk."

Irritated, the billionaire stares at his advisors. They lay claim to fancy law and finance degrees, but they lack the billionaire's business know-how and fire in the belly.

"My whole freaking life has been built on risk," he says. "I spent decades building this company with my sweat and blood, and I deserve compensation in line with elite CEOs. If clients like me never took business risks, you wouldn't be here now, charging your inflated legal fees, would you?"

His voice grows louder.

"You study all of these rules and regs. You have baby-faced associates, not even partners, draft this memo to me. Then you tell me to do *nothing?* I could come up with the same advice for free! I could tell myself to do nothing!"

The billionaire is livid.

"I've shelled out millions of dollars to your firm over the years, and for what? Christ, you just said it *wasn't* illegal. So what's the problem? What am I missing here?"

The billionaire's words burst like buckshot down the hall. If his advisors want to stay with him, they better tweak their advice, he warns. Better yet, trash the advice and write a new memo for him.

"What the hell is wrong with you people?" he screams. "You're gutless, spineless wonders!"

The billionaire stalks out of the conference room, slamming the door behind him. The glass walls quiver. Secretaries look up from their desks.

The grim-faced attorneys purse their lips. For men who bully others in depositions and in court, they are unusually quiet. They gather their papers and close their briefcases.

"The world's richest asshole," the older attorney mutters.

"What now?" a young associate says. "Revise the thing for him?"

"No, we don't change a word. You want the feds in our faces for the next five, six years? We're not signing off on what he wants. If he ignores our advice, he's on his own."

"Are you sure? What'll the managing partners say?"

"I'm a goddamn managing partner. F-ck me."

The billionaire's staff is used to his flare-ups. They are like civilians dropping to the ground during gunfire. When his secretary hears him shouting at his advisors, she looks up, then goes back to work.

The billionaire stomps back into his office and slams the door. He grabs his telephone and throws it across the room. What's the point of having legal advisors if their best advice is no advice?

An hour or two later, he has calmed down. His attorneys left long ago. But they e-mail him to say they will not revise their memo as he requested. They recommend again that he and his company play it safe with their accounting disclosures to regulators.

Sayonara, shit for brains, the billionaire thinks. There are plenty of law firms with more balls.

Everyone has gone home by now. He doesn't see his secretary, but he has told her to stay late.

As the billionaire sits down, he feels a bit woozy. Usually he ignores the discomfort. This time, though, the nausea rises. Sweat covers his forehead, and a rushing sound fills his ears. His heart beats rapid-fire, boom boom boom. A dull pain spreads across his chest.

He crumbles to the ground, striking his head against the side of his desk. He cannot move. He can barely breathe. He tries to cry out, tries to speak, but the pain silences him.

No God, this cannot be happening to me now, my God please don't forsake, he hears his secretary shout, call for help, call 911 she yells.

She runs over to him, curled on the floor. All she can do is loosen his shirt, his tie, his belt so he can breathe more easily. She cradles his head in her hands, wipes his brow and mouth with his handkerchief.

His face contorts in pain, and sweat soaks his blue dress shirt. He feels warm urine on his skin and pants.

His secretary speaks soothingly to him, reassures him, tells him that an ambulance is on its way.

The billionaire's stiff face and body relax a little. His arms drop to the side, and his chest rises and falls. He hears the elevator doors open and the pounding of footsteps.

Paramedics rush into his office. They spray nitroglycerin in his mouth, slap an oxygen mask over his face, and strap him on a gurney. Within minutes, they whisk him down to the parking garage and a waiting ambulance. One of the paramedics recognizes the billionaire.

"Hey, isn't this – "

"Yes, yes, please help him," the secretary says. "Please hurry."

The billionaire cannot move without pain jolting his body.

His head, neck, and chest throb. His mouth and throat are parched. His limbs ache, as if he has the flu. His eyelids feel glued shut.

The billionaire is lucky that his secretary stayed late. If he had been alone, slumped behind his large desk, no one would have seen him until the janitors cleaned up.

"She wanted to go home early," the billionaire says.

"Excuse me?" the doctor says.

"She wanted to leave work early, to spend more time with her church," the billionaire says. "She always joked, 'tick tock, tick tock, life is precious, you should leave early too.' I told her she sounded like a wife. I asked her to stay late, until I got a few things done."

"Then you owe her a bonus," the doctor says, "or at least some time off."

The doctor warns that the billionaire is living dangerously. He needs surgery. Given his age, his heart defect, and his marathon work style, a more severe heart attack is inevitable. Amazingly, x-rays and an electrocardiogram show that his weakened valve has held up over the years.

"Whether you like it or not, we have to fix your ticker as soon as possible," the doctor says. "We didn't go into surgery the other night out of respect for your earlier wishes."

"And my attorneys' wishes," the billionaire says.

"I'm sure they would tell you now to follow our medical advice. They don't want you to die, either. And lose their best client? You should have retired long ago, anyway. You should be touring museums in Europe or something."

"Can't do that, I'm afraid. Got too much business in my blood, and blood in my business."

"So what good are you to your company if you croak? No one cares how much money they make when they're lying on their deathbeds."

"Never heard that one."

"Sarcasm doesn't help, either."

"You don't know what it's like," the billionaire says.

"What, to be filthy rich and arrogant?" the doctor says.

"Funny guy."

"Nurses say I've got the arrogant part down. I'm working on the filthy rich part."

"Cardiologists do okay, I hear."

"Sure, but you could buy this hospital. The whole chain."

"Not quite. You guys are doing well."

"You're doing a lot better, buddy. A billion here, a billion there, pretty soon you've got real – "

"Never heard that one either. I get it."

The doctor grins and pats the billionaire's shoulder.

"Wish I could say you'll be fine, but we have to see you again. You're a land mine ready to go off. Most patients in your position would have met their Makers by now."

"I've taken bigger risks in my time."

"We're talking about your life, not some hedge fund bet. I hope you take care of business and get all of your things in order. This is no joke."

The billionaire mutters thanks, and the doctor leaves. His physician is adamant. He won't take a "No" this time to surgery. The billionaire can straighten out things at work for a couple of days, but then he must return to the hospital. What choice does he have? No choice.

Shaking his head, the billionaire realizes that he has outlived most of his peers, except for a few octogenarian investors on their last deals, and a generation of auto and steel executives who died long ago.

It is one thing to survive the changing of the corporate guard. But he cannot outrun the seasons, his weakening body, his time under heaven.[14]

CHAPTER FOUR

Awakening

"Generous God . . . We praise you for the stories of creation and incarnation, redemption and resolution . . . And we too are a sign of hope for we too hold a story of death and rising, of old and new . . . ."

— "THE HOLY COMMUNION." [15]

AS THE BILLIONAIRE rests in his hospital bed, a young male nurse walks by, whistling Bruno Mars tunes.

The nurse nods at a security guard seated outside the billionaire's private room, and knocks on the half-closed door.

"How you doin' tonight, boss?" the nurse asks. "Need anything? More water, another pillow?"

"Nothing now, thanks."

"You sure? We aim to please."

"I'm fine, thank you."

"You didn't look too good the other night, so they told me to keep an eye on you."

"Appreciate it."

"Hold still while I check everything here. You like music, chief? I can croon some tunes for you. Know a lot of Gershwin and Sondheim, all the standards."

"Not in the mood, pal."

"My girlfriend says I should try out for 'Idol,' but I don't think I'm ready."

"You got that right, Sinatra."

"Hey, boss, you hear the one about the doctor and the billionaire? Doctor tells the billionaire he has a heart condition. Billionaire says he wants a second opinion. Doctor says, 'Okay, you're cheap too.' "

"That's real funny, but not now."

"Hold still, almost done here. Any hot stock tips for me, boss? I don't play the ponies or sports book, but sometimes I take my chances in the market. World's biggest casino, right?"

"Can you let me rest now?" the billionaire says. "I mean it."

"No problem. I got your back, guy. I'm your guardian angel. No silver trumpet, though."

"Appreciate it, Gabe. Now make like a real angel and flap your wings back to the pearly gates."

"You're looking and feeling better already, you know, clowning around and everything. Just ring if you need me. I'll be here until the morning."

The billionaire sighs and shuts his eyes.

The nurse leaves the room, whistling Tony Bennett. There's a whole wing of despondent patients to cheer up.

The task seems endless, but it's the only enjoyable part of his job nowadays, with the cutbacks and extra workload.

Just past the doorway, the nurse looks back at the billionaire.

"Heal thyself, boss," he says. "Heal thyself, and cast thy bread upon the waters." *Ecclesiastes 11:1.*

"What?" the billionaire says. "Hey, pal, what was that?"

In the early evening, the billionaire eats his dinner and watches television. The news has a brief story on him. It sounds like an obituary.

The broadcast lady says there are unconfirmed reports that he suffered a medical emergency, possibly a heart attack, and that an ambulance had rushed him to the hospital. They show an old photo of him, then the well-known photo of him wielding the blowtorch and snarling at the camera.

"He faces possible death at seventy-five," the broadcaster says. "The company would not comment on a succession plan."

A succession plan? The broadcaster hasn't met the billionaire's board of directors. Their succession plan is to promote the guy with the biggest yacht and the prettiest wife or mistress. Now they'll have to do some real work, starting with disclosing his heart ailment to shareholders and regulators.

There is a knock on the door. It's his secretary. A few colleagues and distant relatives send cards and flowers, but she is the only one to visit the hospital.

"How are you feeling?" she asks.

"Everything aches. Not something I want to do again, that's for sure."

"You'll be back in the saddle in no time."

"I owe you thanks. I was lucky you were there."

The nurses have told the secretary that she can stay past visiting hours, if she sits quietly.

"That's awfully kind of you," the billionaire says, "but you should go home."

"I don't mind at all. Your family and friends aren't lining up to see you here. I'll stay for a while, at least until you sleep."

The secretary has brought a bouquet of lilies that she places on his bedside table. She also has brought him some business magazines and the *Wall Street Journal*, but he feels too weak to read. The billionaire notices that she is wearing a blue-and-purple scarf made of silk.

"Pretty scarf," he says.

"Thank you," she says, startled.

The billionaire has to give credit to his secretary. From the start, she has been dutiful and diligent, no matter what. Over the years, she has been sharper, more honest, more reliable than the slugs and losers on his board. And, he admits, she is easier on the eyes than his peers, the same old fraternity of corporate cronies.

How long has she been with him? Longer than most marriages. Through better and worse, the billionaire muses.

When the last global downturn nearly crippled the company and its future looked bleak, many of the billionaire's lieutenants, sensing the company's demise, welcomed calls from headhunters and found new jobs.

But his secretary stayed with the billionaire, lending support and stability during grim times.

"Loyalty isn't a commodity," she told him.

She could care less about his gold-plated balls. A few fiscal quarters later, the company walloped Wall Street estimates and recovered quite nicely.

The secretary puts down the business magazines. In the bedside table, she finds a worn Bible. It is one of those zipper-up Bibles with a black vinyl cover and thin, crinkly pages that tear easily.

She reads a few of her favorite biblical tales and passages. Like listening to hymns or poetry, the verses come back to her, easing her mind. Years later, the words and teachings give solace and sustenance.

The billionaire murmurs and falls asleep. The secretary smiles and smoothes his blanket.

For an hour or two, the billionaire rests quietly. Then, without warning, he sits up gasping and babbling. His face grimaces as he talks. Some of his words are gibberish, while others sound as if he is speaking to someone at his bedside.

He throws off his sheets and tries to get out of bed, but the secretary holds him down.

The billionaire drops his head on the pillow, still dreaming. He tries to clasp his hands in prayer, but he cannot lift them. He starts shouting and babbling again.

"Shhh, it's okay, it's okay," the secretary says.

The male nurse on the night shift looks in.

"Everything okay, ma'am?" he says.

"Yes, we're fine," the secretary says. "I'm sorry, I'll quiet him."

"No problem, ma'am," nurse says. "If he gets worse, I'll come by to help."

The secretary rises from her chair and sits at the billionaire's bedside. She holds his hands, speaks gently to him. Gradually, the billionaire calms down. His voice softens, his face relaxes. She places his limp palms together in prayer.

She opens the Bible and reads more to soothe him. Skimming, she finds *Proverbs 22:9:* "He that hath a bountiful eye shall be blessed, for he giveth of his bread to the poor."

The billionaire drifts asleep again, his chest rising and falling. His hair is wet and matted. He wears a thin blue hospital gown, and a plain blanket and sheet cover him. He looks like every other man on a hospital bed. Weak and lamb-like, shorn of his shorts and a lifetime of conceits.

Nurses chat loudly down the hall. The secretary closes the door.

Maybe it's the late hour, when people do things they normally would not do. Maybe it is seeing the billionaire so vulnerable, lying in bed. Or it may be divinely inspired.

Whatever the cause, the secretary is stirred by a long dormant impulse to help and comfort her ailing boss. It comes as quickly as a flash of anger, as swiftly as the urge to condemn. She is not driven by personal gain or pity. She yearns to give for the sake of giving, to give with no goal or reward. The longing is pure and selfless, and it fills her with devout intensity. The surge of loving kindness wells up from deep within.

The secretary holds the billionaire's hands, strokes his hair and forehead.

"You'll be fine," she says, "everything is fine."

The deep lines in his face relax at her touch. In the warm light, the gray age spots and scabs on his skin seem to fade. Even the battle-hardened edges of his mouth relax, curling into the hint of a baby's smile. His visage looks vastly different from the taut face that the secretary sees in the office.

Whether he can hear her or not, the secretary performs the simplest and most gracious of acts: she gives thanks to the billionaire.

She thanks him for his devotion to his family's business, for honoring the legacies of his father and mother. She thanks him for growing the company over many seasons, like a farmer tending a field, a carpenter building a home.

For all of the billionaire's faults, he has provided for the secretary and others over many years. For all of his cruel and miserly ways, he sustains thousands of workers and their kin. For all of the money that his company makes, most of it goes to paychecks, hospital bills, retirement nest eggs. The billionaire may be beholden to Wall Street, but his honest work has given generations of families the means for shelter, food, clothing. A tabernacle, the secretary thinks.

No one, though, has ever expressed gratitude to the billionaire. He only hears the ugly criticism, the death threats. The secretary knows that his callousness and his knife-like words ward off the lesser attacks, while his wealth shields him from the worst assaults.

"People want their blessings gift-wrapped, but you've given in your own way," she tells him. "People don't realize it, do they? You've been a good shepherd, guiding our company for so long."

The billionaire stirs awake.

"We've been blessed," the secretary says. "We may not show our appreciation. But please know that we're grateful to you for your good works. Thank you for everything."

The billionaire tries to lift his eyelids. His eyes glisten. He wants to thank his secretary, but he cannot talk. He wants to touch her hand, but he cannot move. His body settles into a deep sleep.

The billionaire climbs to the crest of a high hill. Sweating and breathing heavily, he stops to rest. Peering ahead, he sees thick haze covering a small valley.

A dark orange glow filters through the haze. The billionaire spots a brilliant, burning object. It is a large wall of fire, its flames lighting the way.

The billionaire follows the fire's glow to a trail that winds downhill. The trail leads him to the small valley. Acrid smoke fills the air. He passes dry farmlands, charred trees, ponds choked with dead fish.

The trail turns into a paved road snaking to the horizon. The haze lifts, and sunlight breaks through. The billionaire keeps walking. In the distance, he sees a city skyline and plumes of smoke.

The skyline grows larger. As the billionaire nears the city, the high-rise buildings turn crimson. In the flickering light, he sees blood staining the buildings.

Entering the city of blood, the billionaire hears a faint din. The din deepens into a roar. The wall of fire leads to a large public square and a giant bonfire. Flames and black smoke darken the heavens. A vast fortune of gold and silver fills the square.

An epic battle rages between legions of the righteous and the greedy ones. There is much shouting and wailing, the clanging of steel, the pounding of war drums. Horrid cries fill the air. Blood streams from fallen bodies.

The clash surges back and forth, with both sides close to victory, only to see the other side rally and fight back.

After one fierce onslaught, the greedy hordes weaken the ranks of the righteous. Sensing a slaughter, the greedy ones push forward. The righteous warriors fall back, against the giant bonfire. Flames burn them. They scream in agony, and they brace for one last stand.

"No! No!" the billionaire shouts. He races toward the fray to help the righteous.

As the billionaire charges the greedy hordes, a deafening burst of wind and thunder passes over him. The gale strikes all of the warriors. They stop their battle to look up. They are astonished at the sight.

From all quarters of the sky, waves of angels take wing toward the square. Tossing lightning and coals of fire, they descend with a tender fury that frightens the warriors. The angels cut wide paths through the greedy ones, who topple like trees in a storm.

The righteous ones rise to their feet and rally. "Redeem thyself!" they cry out. They roar and charge, beating back the greedy hordes until all have retreated.

The battle ends quickly, amid much howling and wailing. The righteous ones cry out in triumph. As the smoke and flames wane, the victors tend to their wounds and pray for the fleeing horde.

The angels throw into the bonfire all of the treasures that men fight and die for in vain: Mountains of jewelry and coins. Ivory busts and marble thrones. All of the gold, silver, bronze they can find. The angels clear the city for a new kingdom of abundant blessings.

Crossing the battleground, the billionaire sees something glitter. It is near an alley, half-buried under a pile of dirt and debris.

He draws closer to the pile, and clears the debris. He picks up the object. It is the old wedding portrait of his parents, from his home.

What is it doing here? He wipes off the dirt and dust. He runs his fingers over the silver frame and the little gold-plated cross.

Turning over the frame, he gently removes the old photograph, and squints at the back. He sees words in faint black ink, written in graceful, swirling script. He brings the photo closer to his face, to read the writing:

"Dear Son, For what shall it profit a man, if he shall gain the whole world, and lose his own soul? *Mark 8:36.* We Shall Always Love You, Your Father and Mother."

The billionaire kneels on the ground. The words cut through him, cleave his spirit.

His father had warned him long ago. The lessons were clear, but the son had ignored them. His youth and arrogance had blinded him. He had been so foolish, for so long.

In his god-like conceit, had the billionaire squandered his life? Blessed with gifts to last for generations, had he wasted those gifts, spurned those blessings? If he lived for a hundred more years, could he still make amends? Could he take the first steps toward salvaging his soul?

At the depth of his sorrow, the billionaire feels his parents' presence. It is as if they are standing beside him on the edge of the battlefield, embracing him. Their faces smile in approval. Their voices praise and comfort him.

As the righteous ones triumph in the city of blood, the billionaire hears his father and mother with soul-piercing clarity. We are proud of you, son, proud of your good works, *they say.* Come home to us, son, come home.

The billionaire is jolted awake from his reverie.

His heart thumps wildly. His hair and skin are clammy, and sweat drenches his sheets and hospital gown. Soreness and sharp pain still wrack his whole body.

Where is he? Still sleeping and dreaming? He looks around the hospital room, squints at the medical equipment. His secretary is gone.

It is 5 a.m. sharp, a new workweek. Is it Monday or Tuesday? Does it matter? So few hours each day. If the soul of man quickens to creation, he has scant time to waste.

The billionaire shakes his head. Get up, he thinks, get the hell out of bed. He peed in his sleep, so his legs and buttocks are sticky and smelly. He chuckles at his damp underwear. Born pissing, die pissing. From womb to tomb. That pretty much sums up his life. Let's review the key points.

He shuffles to his small bathroom. He dumps his soiled underwear in a bin, and cleans himself. Then he washes his

107

hair in the sink and brushes his teeth. Shaving quickly, he cuts himself with his razor. Like engorged mites, spots of blood ooze on his neck.

His secretary has brought spare clothes – a pressed suit, shirt, and tie, shoes and socks – from the office. He had asked her to bring the files on the new Vietnam deal, but she refused, saying he had to rest.

Rubbing his eyes, the billionaire hobbles to the window. It still is dark. The only view is the parking lot, a grove of trees, a traffic light that blinks green-yellow-red all night. A trash truck rumbles down the street.

The billionaire peers past the parking-lot lights. Past the buildings, the tree line, the foothills. The pre-dawn air is clear and cold. He sees a prayer dome of stars, shimmering, then fading with each breath.

As if on cue, coral bands of light streak across the sky. The bands of light grow longer and wider, refracting from clouds and hills, setting ablaze the landscape. It is an ocean of amber.

My God, the billionaire rarely has seen a more stunning sunrise. He feels as if he could map the terrain, the horizon. He can trace the shrouds of radiant orange light, unfurling from the sky. What was the line from the old English poet? Trailing clouds of glory, he murmurs.[16]

Tick-tock, tick-tock. The billionaire has no time to count grains of sand and God particles. He'll leave the stuff of the universe to poets, prophets, physicists.

His questions are more down-to-earth: If he lost his fabled wealth, trashed his hoard of worldly goods, who would care to remember him? If he gave away his riches to the poorest of the poor, who would listen to his words? Who would love him unconditionally?

Tick-tock, tick-tock. Get dressed, dammit, get the hell out of there.

The billionaire knows that the dawn will fade before most people wake up. If his spirit could reflect this sunrise, for a day or the duration of his life, then he is not ready to die. There still are things that he must do.

CHAPTER FIVE

Convergence

"On the Cross, we bear witness to Christ being forsaken by God . . . Then, in the Resurrection, we discover that God remains, dwelling in our very midst through the embrace of life."

— PETER ROLLINS, *INSURRECTION.*[17]

THE BANKERS STARE at the billionaire as if he is a lunatic. He looks like a wrinkled old specter from another epoch, a spirit clanging chains in the middle of the bank lobby.

It isn't every day that a wealthy client wants to stuff $1 million in crisp $100 bills into a black duffel bag.

The bankers double-check the billionaire's identity. They call the police to make sure he isn't a con artist. They call his company to make sure he isn't the target of kidnappers.

"That's loose change to this guy," the billionaire's senior attorney tells the bankers. "He just had a heart attack a few days ago, so go easy on him."

It isn't easy to convert $1 million in digital money – electronic impulses in giant computers in unmarked buildings hiding the world's most precious data – into real cash. But the bankers do it promptly for the billionaire before the close of banking hours.

"If you don't mind me asking," a banker says, "why do you need so many $100 bills?"

"None of your business," the billionaire says, banging his walking stick on the floor.

"Bank policy – "

"Oh bullshit, just give me my money and report the transaction to Uncle Sam, or I'll take my business to your competitor down the street."

The bank instructs armed security guards to escort the billionaire to his car, but he declines their offer. The guards shake their heads and watch as the billionaire piles the money into his duffel bag. A moment later, one of the bank's richest clients straightens his tie and strolls out the door, carrying a lot of cash.

Walking through the financial district, the billionaire looks like a child on Christmas Eve, eager to rip open his presents. He pulls one stack at a time from the duffel bag. Grabbing several stiff bills, he flings the money into the air.

Some of the $100 bills fall straight to the sidewalk, ignored by people heading home from work. Other bills sail to the street, where cars and buses run over them. Still others ride on gusts past trees and traffic lights.

For the first time since his youth, the billionaire feels joyful and relieved, as if a rock has been lifted from his back. He feels as if he can fly.

"Count thy blessings, people!" he shouts. "Count thy blessings!"

People continue to ignore the billionaire, walking past him and his cash. The sight of a half-crazed man in a suit does not alarm anyone.

But the odd man keeps littering the streets with what some think is play money. Curious, one passerby picks up a bill and crinkles it. She shows her friends, who squint at it in puzzlement.

"Hey, is this real?" she says.

"You know what, it looks real to me," says a friend who is a bank manager. "I think that guy is the billionaire. His office is here, somewhere. What's he doing? Giving away his money?"

Others hear the commotion. They dash toward the billionaire.

"What's going on?"

"Holy shit, is that free money?"

By now, the crowd of followers has grown larger. People scoop and grab the money, then scoop and grab more.

The billionaire looks pleased. He smiles and keeps tossing bills in every direction. He strolls down the street, swinging his walking stick, past wide-eyed office workers, past coffee bars and wine bars, past florists and boutique shops.

"Let not the rich man glory in his riches!" he shouts.

Striding faster, the billionaire passes tourists waiting in lines, shoppers crowding department stores, street people prowling for easy prey. A block or two farther, he tramps past cheap gift shops and liquor stores. The stench of urine and alcohol blends with bus fumes. A multitude of homeless, sprawled on the sidewalk and standing in doorways, stare with glazed red eyes at the billionaire.

Two of the street people, claiming to be military vets of the Iraq War, offer to escort the billionaire through the most dangerous part of downtown. No snipers and hidden explosives on the mean streets. But the muggings, shootings, and body counts are high in the low-rent neighborhood.

"We'll be your private security force," one man says.

The billionaire doesn't tell them about his handgun under his suit, but he welcomes the escort. Past the high-crime zone, he praises the men and gives them fat tips.

"A grateful nation and an old man thank you," he says, saluting.

Huffing, the billionaire reaches a large city park with a fleet of food trucks. White-collar workers enjoy the sun and food inspired by global cuisines. The billionaire draws cheers when he gives $1,000 to each of the food truck vendors, with instructions to pass out free meals to the street people nearby.

"Blessed are the poor in spirit," the billionaire says, "the light of the world." *Matthew 5:3, 5:14.*

Puffing, the billionaire turns toward the civic center and its motley mix of architecture. He strides past the city hall, where his money helps mayors win elections. He passes the symphony hall, where he joins other kingmakers for opening night each season. He waves at the modern art museum, where his gift built a new gallery in the family name.

The flock of people following the billionaire has stalled the traffic. Drivers honk and curse like crazy. The billionaire walks up to the wide-eyed drivers, slips $100 bills into their cars, and thanks them for their patience.

As the crowd swells, the billionaire draws the attention of motorcycle police. One cop keeps the crowd on the sidewalk, while a second cop speeds up to the jabbering rich guy.

"Sir, we have to ask you to stop handing out cash," the officer says. "You're blocking traffic, causing all kinds of problems. People are getting into fistfights back there."

"I'm sorry, officer, I'll stop now," the billionaire says. "I can keep walking, though?"

"Yeah, you can keep going if the crowd doesn't get larger. Just don't throw all that cash into the streets. Write a check to charity or something."

"Got it, officer, thank you."

The billionaire walks and walks.

Sweating and breathing heavily, he treks to a tony district for the rich and powerful. The neighborhood, resting on the crest of a high granite hill, offers dramatic views of the harbor, the bay, the bridge. The billionaire can smell the wealth and power. Financiers here, politicians there. Wealthy oil heirs. Internet billionaires. Old and new money galore. He strides past many mansions, many consulates.

His heart pounding, the billionaire pauses to rest. Catching a second wind, he stands up and treks down the steep hill, almost stumbling on the sidewalk, to a street of stylish bars and restaurants, where young professionals dream of wealth so they, too, can live in fancy hilltop homes.

The billionaire's head throbs. His strides slow. Crossing more streets, he finally reaches the water.

His crowd of followers has thinned. He has walked far, and given away nearly all of his money, so a lot of people have lost interest in the cavalcade. The motorcycle police speed off to a drunk-driving crash.

Near the water's edge, the billionaire walks past a forest of sailboat masts, past a fancy yacht club and a corporate party in full swing. Past picnickers and volleyball players on the beach. Past families enjoying the spring day and late-afternoon sun.

He trudges in the sand past small dunes and marshes, toward the harbor bridge a short hike away. He can look down at the bridge from his hillside home. But the sweeping vista from the beach – the lofty steel structure and golden brown hills, the indigo ocean and clear azure sky – makes him pause and give thanks each time he sees it.

Small waves surge onshore, wetting the billionaire's shoes and suit. He yells and runs into the waves, kicking and splashing. He cups his hands, flings water and wet sand into the air.

A waist-high wave hits him, knocking him off balance. He falls to his hands and knees, dropping his walking stick. He laughs and dunks his head in the water, then stands and shakes his body like a wet dog.

The billionaire trots back to the beach. Hearing an imagined symphony, he holds out his arms and waltzes with himself in the wet sand.

Faint and wobbly, he falls again.

A young mother, no older than 17 or 18, toddles by with her little boy.

"Look at that old man, getting all wet in his clothes," says the mother, zipping her faded sweatshirt. "I think that's the millionaire. They just talked about him on the radio. He's a millionaire, baby. Like on the TV game shows."

"Where, Mama?"

"Right over there."

The little boy giggles and runs toward the old man, who stands slowly.

"Hey, come back here!" the mother says.

The little boy jumps in the waves, up to his waist. He shrieks and splashes water on the old man, who laughs and splashes back. The little boy picks up the billionaire's walking stick and hands it to him.

"Why thank you, young man! Here, I have a gift for you," the billionaire says, handing the kid several soaked $100 bills. "Give it to your family."

The little boy runs back to his mother, who gasps in disbelief.

"Look, look, he gave me money!" the boy says. "He gave me a million dollars! I have a million dollars, Mama!"

Nearing the bridge, arcing high over the harbor strait, the billionaire hurls almost the last of his $100 bills.

The money flutters through the air, alighting in cattails, dune grass, wildflowers. A recent spring rain has given life to dry roots. A few bills get blown into the tide. People whoop and shout as they stomp through the sand, chasing the cash.

Near the base of the bridge, the billionaire cranes his neck to stare at the wingspan of steel beams and cables. Looming above are the bridge's colossal, slate gray towers, flanking each other like sentries.

Feeling nauseous and lightheaded, the billionaire sits cross-legged to catch his balance. He shivers and sheds his wet coat and tie, leaving them on the ground.

After resting, the billionaire rises to his feet. Breathing deeply, he climbs a trail up a steep hill to the bridge. He passes fireweed, blackberries, poison oak. Red-tailed hawks soar among gaunt pine and eucalyptus trees, its bark peeling like lepers' skin. Ground squirrels dash for cover. A

Peregrine falcon dives to the dank forest floor, grabs its bloodied prey, and flies back to the treetops for a last meal before dark.

At the top of the trail, the billionaire rests by the entrance to the bridge's sidewalk.

Feeling better, he starts crossing the bridge to the roar of traffic and the smell of ocean air. Thousands of commuters speed by, heading for home. A new crowd of onlookers follows him on foot. Police and news helicopters circle overhead, and reporters on the ground race to catch up to the man.

Some of the commuters have seen the CEO-turned-saint on the news. They honk and wave at the mad mogul, his new media nickname. Music blares from car stereos. *Don't let some hell-bent heart leave you bitter,* Lee Ann Womack sings.[18] On radio talk shows, callers say the billionaire has revived their faith in mankind in a world that worships money and status.

Some drivers honk and shout in support of the billionaire's largesse.

"You da Man, billionaire!"

"God bless you!"

He shouts back, waving. "Thou shall love with all thy heart, all thy soul!"

The billionaire reaches the bridge's mid-span, as high as skyscrapers. The roadbed rumbles under him. He feels as if he is awakening from a vivid dream that goes on in real life.

He leans against the railing, arms outstretched. The fading sun glows through the rolling mist. A foghorn blasts as ships pass below. Cold air, sweeping south from the Arctic, cleanses his lungs. He sees the city skyline, shining as dusk falls. He turns to the ocean, the infinite darkness.

The billionaire's heart weakens with each step. A dull and heavy ache spreads across his chest. The nausea comes again, filling his mouth and throat with bile.

He has ignored his doctor's warnings, and the urging of his secretary. Despite their good intentions, he does not wish to prolong – by surgery or technology – what remains of his frail life. He has no dependents or close relatives. He believes, rightly or wrongly, that his work and his calling are finished for now. His wealth, he knows, will go far.

The old man stands motionless by the bridge railing. He shivers, neither alive nor dead. Fog coils around the bridge towers. It seems fitting, given his family's calling in global commerce, that the billionaire's life pilgrimage might end overlooking the sea.[19]

The billionaire tosses his walking stick. Slowly, he raises his leg and lifts himself up to the railing. He climbs atop the railing, sitting astride it like a beam of wood. His body feels heavy, as if encased in stone. Ignoring the pain, he pumps his fists for the crowd.

The onlookers cheer. They think they're watching the filming of a TV commercial or a reality show. Elderly bystanders recall the old *The Millionaire* show, and wonder if this is a modern remake. When the news cameras aim at spectators, they wave and scream for their brief seconds of fame.

"Preach, billionaire!" someone shouts.

"I will tell you that we have not been forgotten!" the billionaire hollers, his voice weakening. "I swear to you, we have not been forsaken!"

A local broadcast reporter, trailing the billionaire from downtown, squeezes between onlookers to get closer to the man. Is he putting on a show for the masses, or trying to end his life?

The reporter has covered many gruesome news stories, seen many mangled and bloodied bodies. In car and plane crashes. In fires, floods, earthquakes. At homicide and mass murder sites. At mortuaries and the coroner's office.

There is no glory in clay-like corpses drained of blood, embalmed for burial. Nearly all of the people who fall from high bridges endure horrific deaths when they slam at high speeds into the concrete-hard water. As if struck by a giant sledgehammer, the body's organs burst into a mass of blood and tissue.

There is no sacrament in suicide, he thinks. Only sadness and grief. Surely the billionaire's passing would hurt his loved ones, just as his living would spare them pain.

Please don't jump, the reporter thinks, please hang on. Talk to someone who can help you, who can console you.

The billionaire suddenly swings his legs over the railing, then steps down to a narrow outer ledge barely a foot wide.

"Wait, don't!" the reporter yells. "Let's talk for a minute!"

Faint voices call out to the billionaire, standing treacherously on the ledge. A strong gust or a slip would send him plunging off the bridge.

Sirens wail from fire trucks and police cars. Onlookers beg the billionaire to get down.

"Please don't jump!" a woman yells. "Think of all you can do for others!"

"Jump, you bastard!" shouts a passing driver. "Think of all the lives you've trashed!"

In the traffic and crowd of onlookers, Good Samaritans are outshouted by cynics. The users, the takers, the doubters. Upset that the billionaire has run out of cash, they jeer at him as he straddles the railing.

A bystander begs: "You got more money there? I need to feed my kids, man! Come on, I got a family to feed!"

A truck driver slows and throws a soda can at the billionaire, barely missing him.

"Hey, Gatsby, take a flying leap!" he shouts. "One less greedy asshole in the world!"

Another driver chimes in. "You can give away all your money, but you can't save yourself!"

The billionaire grabs the last bunch of $100 bills from his pants pocket.

"Here, is this what you want?" he shouts, waving the bills.

The billionaire flings the cash into the air. People rush toward him. Some dive to the sidewalk to grab the money. Others run to the railing, reaching for the bills as they swirl out of reach. Several lean too far and almost fall, before others grab their clothes and yank them back.

Police and firemen race to the scene. They push back the crowd, then cautiously approach the billionaire. They ask how he is doing, how they can help him. Talk to us, buddy, talk to us, one says. We've got your back, boss.

The billionaire cannot hear the voices, muted by the wind and traffic. His heartbeat pounds in his ears. He turns to glance at the gleaming city. He senses his father and mother's presence, and he says a prayer in remembrance.

The billionaire smiles weakly at the crowd. Who are these strangers? He wishes that he could help them, tend to them. People want hope and faith more than anything, he thinks. Would his death sadden them? Or would his gifts inspire them for a moment or two? He knows that all – rich or poor, young or old – have gifts to be unearthed and shared.

Moments pass. Clutching the railing with both hands, the billionaire wobbles on the ledge, as if wondering what to do. He leans back and forth, unsure whether to step back to the sidewalk, or step into the sky.

His face is pale and ashen. The long trek to the bridge has drained him. His arms and legs weaken. His hands are cold and numb. He cannot grip the railing much longer.

Without warning, a breath of wind from the ocean washes over the billionaire. The gust steadies him, holds him still against the railing. It shields him from the chill, warms his limbs, lifts his spirit.

The billionaire closes his eyes, giving in to a painful joy that he has never felt before. It is a deep and aching bliss that consumes him, burns through him. The sweet anguish and awe flood through his body, nearly driving him to his knees. A light shines through the mist, blinding him for a moment, but he is afraid to turn away.

He mourns all that he has lost, and exalts all that he will gain. In giving without end, he hopes to uplift others. In seeking forgiveness, he hopes to uplift himself. To converge beyond hatred and joy, beyond sorrow and bliss. He longs to love wholly, to give selflessly, at the moment of embarking when his heart gives way to the divine.

He seeks undying deliverance and devotion. To live again, to begin again, with a sense of wonder commensurate to his capacity for giving.

Yes, he believes that he still has much to offer in his lasting years. He can guide and teach others, give more of himself. There is so much to pass on while he has the strength. *Make me an instrument of Thy peace, for it is in giving that we receive.*

A surge of adrenalin rips through him, ending his reverie. To the cheers of onlookers, the billionaire lifts a leg off the ledge and tries to pull himself up.

123

"Come on, you can do it!" people shout. "You can do it!"

He struggles to climb back on the railing, to get down to the sidewalk, but his arms and legs shake violently. He cannot hold on.

The rescuers rush to grab him.

"Hold on, we've got you, pal," one says.

The billionaire looks toward his rescuers. But before they can reach him, his face grimaces. His body stiffens like a rod. The crowd cannot hear his heart shudder and seize up.

The pain comes from everywhere. His jaw feels as if an iron vise has clamped tight. He feels buried neck-deep in mud and concrete that crushes his chest. Almost blacking out, he imagines a flaming sword from the mist falling toward him, cleaving his flesh and bone. The pain nearly shears the spirit from his body.

It takes a second or two for witnesses to grasp what is going on. Was that real? Did that really happen? Oh my God no, he just fell off the bridge, he slipped off the bridge. Call for help, hurry someone, call for help.

A little girl, sitting on her father's shoulders, looks on in fear and wonder.

"Daddy, did you see that man?" she says. "Did you see him?"

The broadcast reporter looks over the railing, unsure whether the billionaire was trying to save his life or save his soul.

The reporter sees a small figure falling silently, as if in slow motion. The figure seems to stand on the ocean air, almost floating. From a distance, the body looks serene and still, as the wind carries it downward.

In truth, the billionaire tumbles through the air, his terror swelling each second. The wind whips his body back and forth, like trash on the beach. Shouts and screams ring from the bridge. More sirens wail in the distance.

As the billionaire plunges toward the white-capped waters, he panics even more. He thrashes his limbs in the air, as if drowning. Dizzy and disoriented, he cannot think, cannot breathe. A slab of cold air crushes his chest, forcing the breath from him. He feels frozen, helpless. Darkness starts to take hold of him.

All of a sudden, the cold air rolls away. The heaviness lifts from his chest. He chokes and struggles for breath, gasps again and again. The darkness ebbs. He can see the water and harbor.

A wave of warmth enfolds his body, bracing him for his passing. He falls gently through the sky.

The bountiful waters rise to meet him. He is struck by the finality, the eternity, of this last act under the sun. Tears cleanse and burn his stricken face. *Into thine hands . . . Upon the face of the waters.* He lifts his arms skyward, in a gesture akin to hope and faith.

As screams echo from the bridge, the billionaire's body slams into the bay. It sounds like a muted thunderclap, a distant pop, and then quiet.

Seconds after falling from the bridge, the limp body bobs in the water like a broken little mannequin, head twisted, arms and legs akimbo.

A Coast Guard patrol boat races across the choppy harbor. The rescuers know that nearly all who fall from the bridge die of blunt trauma and drowning, although a few miraculously survive. The boat slows as it nears the body, floating face down in the swift current.

"That puppy's gone to heaven," says one rescuer.

"Check him closely anyway," another says. "You never know."

Sailboats and ships pass by, returning to their berths. No one sees the body in the darkening light. Or they see it, but they do not care to care.

On the bridge, drivers sit stuck in traffic, blasting their horns, bleating on cell phones. Life races on. Nothing changes.

And yet . . . .

All of the boats, the helicopters, the bridge's security cameras do not capture it. It happened so quickly. No one really knows for sure. Not the rescuers, not the news reporters, not the onlookers.

In their statements to the police, who have heard much stranger things over the years, several people say they saw something very odd, very surreal. It was like a Hollywood movie, they say.

126

They swear that the man's body, before it struck the water like a plane slamming into the ground, actually seemed to *slow* for a second or so.

Yes, they saw it, the onlookers tell the skeptical cops. They swear on the Bible, on their mothers' graves. It was the freakiest thing, they say. It felt like a dream, a nightmare. No, they aren't crazy. Do they look crazy? He was the guy giving away a million bucks to strangers.

As people watched from the bridge, they could not turn their eyes from the sight. The man was flailing wildly, like leapers from burning buildings.

Then, near the end of the fall, he seemed to settle down and start to slow, as if floating in the frigid air.

To some, he appeared to be gliding like a bird for a breath or two. The calming ocean winds swathed the man, lifted him above the still and forgiving waters. Like a raptor or a dove at play, winging silently across the bay.

Before the billionaire struck the water, some say they glimpsed an essence, a kind of luminescence, streaming from his waif-like body. It was a brilliant and tender light. As sure as the next dawn, the onlookers swear that the man's soul was arcing skyward.

My God, one witness says, it was as if he was rising to grace.

Epilogue

THE ATTORNEY AND the executor toss their coffee cups and look at their watches.

"Did you catch the news this morning?" the attorney says.

"Only a few minutes. I had to run."

"He's been on every network for days. One of the broadcasters said, 'It's the gospel according to Saint Billionaire! Be grateful, not hateful! He died, so others might give!' Christ, he's gone from the world's richest asshole to Saint Francis of Assisi. We're never gonna hear the end of it."

"Don't worry, it'll die down soon," the executor says. "All of this shouldn't take too long to unwind."

The executor and the attorney greet the secretary in the lobby of their downtown law offices. After small talk, they invite her to a conference room and hand her a copy of the billionaire's will. Given his wealth, his will is reasonably clear and simple.

The billionaire did not wish to be buried at a gravesite that would crumble and soon be forgotten. He requested a cremation, his ashes spread at sea.

To the dismay of his distant relatives on conference call, the billionaire leaves them only a few million dollars each –

just enough to placate their greed. If they challenge his will because they think that he committed suicide, the billionaire's attorneys will wage an all-out legal counter-attack.

To the surprise of his employees and their labor unions, the billionaire gives $1 billion to job-training programs at local trade and business schools. The blowtorch-wielding maintenance man, plus thousands of workers axed by the billionaire, will receive financial aid. Some of them will be rehired during the next economic boom. If their children go to college, the billionaire's money will pay their tuition and housing.

To the delight of his secretary, the billionaire has bestowed his last $1 billion to a global foundation devoted to education and health care for the poorest of the poor. Other donors have given much more. But because of his tragic death and his $1 million give-away to strangers, the billionaire's gift reaps worldwide media attention, and it shines more light on altruistic capitalism.

Lastly, the billionaire leaves a generous gift to his closest advisor.

The secretary sits silently, in disbelief, when the executor says that the billionaire has given her $100 million in cash and company stock.

Did she hear correctly? The executor said $100 million? The news shocks her. No, this cannot be happening, she thinks. It seems unreal, dream-like. Her face flushes hot. The room seems to shimmer and float.

"I'm sorry, I feel faint," she says.

The attorney gives the secretary a cup of water. Her mouth and throat are parched. She sips slowly.

"He wanted you to have the money," the executor says, "because you were the most loyal, trustworthy person in his life. He knew that you wouldn't hurt the company or squander his financial gift, long after his death.

"Most of the investors who flew into town cared only about making a quick killing on their investments. He said only you and a handful of loyalists cared about the long-run health of the company and its employees.

"He said you were smarter and worked harder than half of the jackasses – his word, not mine – on the company's board. You were the most ethical and well-organized manager he had ever seen. His business life would have been a near disaster without you, and he thought you deserved part of his wealth.

"When we asked him if he wanted to give such a large amount to a person outside of family, he joked that you were like a spouse or a daughter to him. He said, 'Better a poor and wise child then an old and foolish king' " *Ecclesiastes 4:13.*

To the secretary's amazement, the billionaire also left instructions to his loyal executives to place her on the management fast track, just as his father had done for him long ago. If all went well, she could succeed him as CEO in a year or two. Until then, the loyalists would run the company.

The billionaire had anticipated an uprising from the disgruntled directors, who were nearly as arrogant and covetous as he had been.

Corporate security had confirmed his secretary's suspicions that the directors were plotting a coup. The billionaire's company, despite its steady growth, had lost ground to quicker competitors in recent years. So the dissidents felt that it was their fiduciary duty to fire the billionaire, and to find a younger CEO with a yen for more sizzling stock performance.

To quell the rebellion, the billionaire had told his attorneys and loyal investors to oust the directors at the next shareholders' meeting, and to clear the path for his secretary to rise to power.

If the dissidents and key shareholders fight back, the billionaire's cadre of loyal investors will launch a furious takeover battle that will not last long. The loyalists – ethical and socially responsible funds in the United States, Europe, Asia, and Latin America – already have quietly joined forces.

The dissident directors do not know about this powerful phalanx of global investors. But it was the fiduciary duty of the billionaire to inform them from his grave.

"He wasn't proud of everything he did," the executor says. "But he said that he wanted his last corporate battle to be a just and righteous one."

The secretary feigns surprise about the coup. She had seen it taking shape months ago, before telling the billionaire. The secretary knows the boardroom machinations and personalities – the loyal and disloyal players, the honest and unethical ones – better than any one.

From her desk, she has seen treachery and greed-driven acts of all kinds. Sadly, the greedy acts outnumber the acts of corporate altruism and good works.

Coughing, the executor checks his notepad.

"One last thing," he says. "He left another large gift, up to $100 million over ten years, for your church to use for worthy social and educational programs.

"His only condition is that the project must be named after your late father. He deeply regretted not paying his respects at the memorial service, and he has arranged for lilies to be placed at your father's gravesite each Sunday, until you've passed away."

The secretary shakes her head. The billionaire's gift and the CEO succession plan for her surely are heaven-sent. She saw no signs that he had believed so devoutly in her. He had kept his largesse hidden deep within him, until the end.

"I had no idea," the secretary says.

The executor says that the secretary can do anything she wants with her money. Buy a yacht, buy a mansion, fly around the world. The executor and the attorney laugh, say how lucky she is, then tell her to see her accountant.

The secretary knows what she will do with her financial windfall.

She will pay off her mortgage and make sure she is set for retirement. She will take her pastor and church volunteers to a nice dinner, and maybe treat herself to a vacation. She'll give most of the gift to her church to renovate its chapel and its home for the elderly, and to fund the church's ailing poverty program.

She will ponder the CEO position, a golden opportunity. As the billionaire's proxy for so long, the secretary boasts a wealth of experience and inside knowledge that would come into play in the new job.

The executor and the attorney look over the billionaire's will one last time.

The secretary interrupts them.

"What happened up there?" she asks.

"Pardon?"

"The bridge. Was he trying to commit suicide?"

"Oh God no, we don't think so. To our knowledge, he seemed perfectly fine and sound of mind. When we met to revise his will, he was in good spirits. He even had a couple of new deals that he was eager to take on.

"When he led that little parade through the city, we think it was a publicity stunt, a brilliant marketing move. On the bridge, the police and every witness said he was trying to climb down from the barrier, but his heart gave out.

"Having said that, we know that his health was failing badly, and he had refused surgery. He had no dependents or close loved ones. He may have thought he had accomplished all that he could, and he wanted to leave a legacy."

"No note or warning signs?"

"Not to our knowledge. You were his executive assistant. You saw him every day, right? Even when he gave away $1 million to strangers, there was nothing wrong with that. People lose fortunes all the time on Wall Street.

"It's hard to know what he was thinking. We couldn't read his mind, or his soul. It's like asking someone whether he or she believes in God. For some, it's a very private question. Whatever the case, I hope his prayers were answered."

"I wish he had said something. I could have talked to him. I could have helped him."

"We're very sorry."

"No, thank you for everything. I'll get back to you soon on the CEO succession."

"By next week?"

"As soon as I can. I'll let you know. Please let me know immediately if anything else comes up."

"Yes, we will, ma'am."

The secretary steps from the law offices into the late-morning light. Still dazed by the news, she walks toward the harbor. She sits on a grassy patch near the water, in the warm sun.

She rubs the ring on her finger. It has become her good-luck amulet, an emblem of her parents' unending love and best wishes for her.

They were right. Her father and mother were right.

134

They knew that people each day transcend greed and self-interest to perform extraordinary acts of kindness. They knew that grieving can open gateways to good works full of meaning and purpose. They knew that faith from within can lead to greater faith in others.

How had the secretary failed to see the billionaire's ailing spirit? Why had she not reached out to him?

She kneels on the ground, ignoring the traffic and pedestrians. Cradling herself, she rocks back and forth. She cries softly at first, then in rising waves of sorrow.

Who knoweth the spirit of man that goeth upward? She asks for forgiveness. Forgiveness, for her vanity and blindness. Forgiveness, for damning and distrusting others. Forgiveness, for doubting her faith.

In praise, in gratitude, she thanks the billionaire for his benevolence and his final acts of grace. She prays for his soul's safe deliverance, as he bears his many burdens and wheels his way toward heaven.

She lifts her arms, cups her trembling hands to the sky, in a gesture akin to hope and belief.

"Rejoice," she cries out, "rejoice."

Author's Note

THANKS VERY MUCH for reading *The Billionaires Gift* and for supporting all digital and traditional writers, publishers, and bookstores. Readers keep alive our craft, and your support and patronage are deeply appreciated.

If you enjoyed *The Billionaire's Gift* and *Fusion Entrepreneurs*, my business ebook on globalization, please consider adding a brief customer's comment or mini-review on my pages at Amazon.com.

If you would like to subscribe to my blog or receive an e-mail alert when my next book is released, please visit and sign up at *CoolGlobalBiz.com.* Your email stays private, it will not be sold or shared with anyone, and you can unsubscribe if you so choose.

I can be reached at info@EdwardIwata.com, on Twitter @EdwardIwata, or on LinkedIn (if you are a LinkedIn user).

For *The Billionaire's Gift,* thank you to: KitFosterDesign in Edinburgh, Scotland, for the evocative cover art. BookDesignTemplates in Marin County, California, for the professional e-book design. The Peninsula Writers Group for the monthly lunches and lively talks. The Writer's Digest West 2012 conference in Los Angeles for the valuable hands-on advice. The National Novel Writing Month online project (NaNoWriMo) for providing structure and events for writers. And thanks to all at the vanguard of the e-book and indie self-publishing revolution. I hope that hybrid models emerge that benefit everyone.

Much gratitude, of course, to family and ancestors, friends and coworkers, teachers and fellow writers, for your support. We're the products of all who came before us, and I would not be here without your help, advice, and knowledge. I've thanked many in *Fusion Entrepreneurs,* and my apologies to anyone I've omitted.

Most of all, in a crazed and chaotic world, I'm grateful to God and Buddha for helping many of us find a higher purpose in life. *The Billionaire's Gift* is about seeking one's calling. There is no doubt in my mind that everyone in a free society can choose our destinies and cultivate our talents. Each of us – rich and poor, young and old – can bear a gift to share with others.

A recent personal episode – one of many signs that appeared while I wrote *The Billionaire's Gift* – confirmed my belief that I've rediscovered my true purpose as a writer, after decades of cranking out news stories.

The day before I planned to publish *The Billionaire's Gift*, something unknowable compelled me and my wife to attend an early Sunday morning service at Grace Cathedral, an Episcopal church in San Francisco that welcomes all faiths. I had not visited the church for decades, and it was a long drive from our home and our warm, cozy bed.

At the time, I was wrestling with serious stage fright at the launch of my fiction debut. It was an unusual feeling for me; nerves had never stopped me from seeking my goals. As a journalist, I was fearless when covering big news stories, or diving into business and political investigations. I was swimming in my element.

But as a fiction writer, I felt shakier. The thought of unveiling my first novella – especially on spiritual themes – made my palms sweat and my pulse race. I had felt the same way at 18, when I parachuted out of a plane with college pals. Tossed by the wind, I had landed awkwardly and crunched several vertebrae. Luckily, I wasn't crippled.

Every writer goes through the same self-doubts. What if no one likes our books? What if months or years of hard work go to waste? In my case, what if my tale of a greed-driven billionaire seeking a higher purpose misses the mark? What if it fails to reflect the spirit of the times? In an era of godless materialism, do people even care about the quest for meaning in our lives and careers?

As it turned out, the guest speaker at Grace Cathedral that day was Jon McCormack, an executive at Amazon's Lab 126 and co-founder of the Kilgoris Project, a nonprofit that builds schools and offers healthcare and clean water to thousands of children in rural Kenya.

His topic: God and technology. According to McCormack, more technologists in his world seem to be seeking greater meaning in their lives, beyond the corporate grind and entrepreneurial dreams of striking it rich.

After his talk, the cathedral's Very Reverend Dr. Jane Shaw delivered a similar moving message to the large congregation. In her sermon, she urged everyone to seek connections and to care for others and the planet, rather than blindly chase money and material goods.

To my relief, the spiritual themes that the reverend and the executive touched on that Sunday mirrored the themes of *The Billionaire's Gift*. For me, it was more affirmation that my leap into fiction-writing wasn't a blind leap of faith.

For sure, I could have spared myself a lot of grief by being a good little journalist. I could have confirmed that the age-old quest for a higher calling still is relevant for people of all faiths and followings. I could have hounded experts, dug up public-opinion surveys, combed through much literature.

But that was the last thing I wanted to do with this story. I had no wish to vet my spiritual beliefs in the same way I vetted business gurus and high-flying stocks. I had no desire to document, with a reporter's feeble tools, what ultimately is infinite and immeasurable. I wanted to live my faith in the world, not dissect it to death.

Was the Grace Cathedral episode just a coincidence? Or was it a divine tap on the shoulder, reminding me to stay the course, to ignore cynics, to believe in myself and my work?

In the end, can we prove beyond all doubt that we're pursuing the right callings in our lives? That's a question to be answered by each of us, in fellowship or pilgrimage, or in the privacy of our thoughts and prayers. Ultimately, mapping one's destiny remains an intensely personal journey. There are no guarantees.

But if we embark on our new callings with undoubting faith and belief, I'd like to think that someone on high will give us plenty of guidance.

— Edward Iwata
Spring, 2013

End Notes

---

[1] Elie Wiesel, "Nobel Peace Prize Acceptance Speech," Oslo, Norway, 1986.

[2] Ne-Yo, "CNN Heroes" broadcast and CNN.com transcript, 2012.

[3] Remarks of Bill Gates, Harvard Commencement 2007, Harvard Gazette, June 7, 2007.

[4] The "Peace Prayer" often is attributed to Saint Francis of Assisi, the Catholic saint in the thirteenth century who took a vow of poverty to devote his life to God. But according to history professor Christian Renoux at the University of Orleans in France, the prayer first appeared anonymously in 1912 in *La Clochette,* a publication of The Holy Mass League.

[5] Echoing T.S. Eliot's "The Love Song of J. Alfred Prufrock" (1917).

[6] Alluding to Percy Bysshe Shelley's "Ozymandias" (1818).

[7] All of the biblical verses in this story come from The Project Gutenberg EBook of the *King James Bible*, EBook #10, under a Project Gutenberg License (2011).

[8] "Price Tag" (Island Records, 2011), a global megahit performed by Jessie J and written by Jessie J, B.o.B., Dr. Luke, and Claude Kelly.

[9] Mitch Albom quoted Morrie Schwartz, his late teacher in *Tuesdays With Morrie* (New York: Doubleday and Random House, 1977), at the Cathedral of Faith in San Jose, California, U.S.A., in 2011. Albom is the author of *The Five People You Meet in Heaven* (New York: Hyperion, 2003), and other books on spiritual themes.

[10] Controversial original lyrics from the hymn "All Things Bright and Beautiful" by Mrs. Cecil Frances Alexander in 1858. (See: various publishers' editions of *Hymns Ancient and Modern* and also Elizabeth M. Knowles, *Oxford Book of Quotations*, Oxford: Oxford University

Press, 1999.) The original lyrics, which some believe espoused a class system of inequality, were banned by the London Education Authority in 1982. (See: Rupert Christiansen, "The Story Behind the Hymn," *The Telegraph*, September 22, 2007.)

[11] Leonard Cohen, "Anthem" (Stranger Music Inc., Columbia, Sony Music Entertainment, 1992).

[12] John Ciardi translation of Dante Alighieri's *The Paradiso* (New York: New American Library, 1970), Canto XXIX, lines 65-66.

[13] T.S. Eliot, *The Complete Poems and Plays* (New York: Harcourt, Brace and Company, 1930).

[14] Echoing Ecclesiastes 3:1-8: "To every thing there is a season, and a time to every purpose under the heaven . . . ."

[15] "The Holy Communion" was recited Christmas Eve 2012 at Stanford Memorial Church at Stanford University, California, U.S.A. It was adapted from a communion liturgy at Iona Abbey, Scotland.

[16] William Wordsworth's "Ode: Intimations of Immortality from Recollections of Early Childhood" (1807). Wordsworth writes that the soul, "our Life's Star," trails "clouds of glory…from God, who is our home."

[17] Peter Rollins, *Insurrection: To Believe Is Human, To Doubt, Divine* (New York: Howard Books / Simon & Schuster, 2011), p. 160. A brilliant contemporary view of Christ's resurrection.

[18] "I Hope You Dance" (MCA Nashville, 2000), by Lee Ann Womack, Mark Daniel Sanders, and Tia Sillers, is one the most inspiring hit songs of recent years.

[19] Echoing William Wordsworth's "Resolution and Independence," (1807), in which a gray-haired old man stands motionless by a moor, near the end of his "life's pilgrimage."

143

20475854R00085

Made in the USA
Charleston, SC
15 July 2013